About the

Margaret Armstrong lives in County Durham, having spent much of her adult life in the south-east. Her many and varied jobs include piano teacher, secretary, life and pensions rep, upholsterer and, at one period of her life, she worked as a one-woman cottage industry producing and selling handmade bags. The mother of four grown-up children, Margaret has been writing both poetry and short stories from a very early age. This is her debut novel.

Bury me not in the arms of the yew
For fear of unquiet rest
Lie me with wildflowers, laden with dew
Rich earth upon my breast
Where eternal sleep will heal my sorrow
Where arising cannot be
Then I will not come upon the morrow
To vent my wrath on thee

THE YEARNING OF THE YEW

Margaret Armstrong

THE YEARNING OF THE YEW

Vanguard Press

A CIP catalogue record for this title is
available from the British Library.

ISBN 978-1-80016-373-7

*Vanguard Press is an imprint of
Pegasus Elliot MacKenzie Publishers Ltd.*
www.pegasuspublishers.com

First Published in 2022

**Vanguard Press
Sheraton House Castle Park
Cambridge England**
Printed & Bound in Great Britain

Dedication

In dedication to my much loved and missed parents, Tommy and Nancy, and in memory of my dear brother, David. You remain forever in my thoughts.

Acknowledgements

I'll be forever grateful for the support and encouragement of my four children, and for the faith my brother, and fellow writer, John, has in me and which never wavers. Thank you so much. My thanks also to Lorraine and Alan, who have supported me throughout this process, to Brian for his excellent photography, and to the very kind and helpful staff of Consett Library, who gave me the space to work when needed.

Preface

The night air is still. The grass stands stiff and crisp under the twinkle of the hoar frost. At the edge of the meadow stands a lone tree. Twisted and gnarled. Ancient. Nothing stirs. The owl does not hoot. The night creatures cease their rustling, loath to risk exposure under the glare of a full moon. Silence. A watcher might have sensed a whisper. A susurration. A rustle of leaves. A call to resurrection. *Time*, breathe the branches. The whisper travels from leaf to twig. From twig to branch. Trunk to root. Two sighs come from below. From within the mulched earth. Disturbing the frost. Shaking its powder from the toxic tips of the sharpened leaves. Revealing the green gloss. But there was no watcher. No one to witness the awakening.

***

We've been waked, Pickie. It's almost time. She's kept her promise. Gettin' us ready. We've been rested long while she put her strength in us. Her desire. Our need. Prepared us for what's to come. What's necessary. Our keeper has need of bolsterin' her mournin.' Bones keeps her thrivin.' She's found them. They'll soon be here and we're ready to do her biddin'. And her biddin' is our biddin'. She's doin' it for us, Pickie. She's the one who's shown us the love we never thought to have.

Chapter One

'What do you think then?' Martin had looked up from his half-eaten creme brulee. 'It really is a great opportunity.'

'Like maybe going back to your roots? What are you? Some sort of homing pigeon?' Beth teased. 'That's where your family originated from, isn't it? Up north?'

'Somewhere up there, as you know well enough. The same way you know that my family history is a bloody great mystery, to say the least. I've told you as much as I've been able to find out. Best forgotten, apparently, according to my poor dead mother. Stuffed under the carpet! Not to be mentioned! Any time the subject of ancestry came up, lips were clamped shut and they stayed that way.'

'And you never found out why? No clues at all?'

'Didn't really pursue it after a while. Gave up. Eventually realised I didn't really care that much. Especially as my mother would go into a state of apoplexy every time her family history was brought up. Resentment and disappointment oozed out of her every pore, as it did from her mother as well. I tell you, Beth, you could almost taste the bitterness. All I was able to gather from the reluctant, almost monosyllabic answers to my few and far between questions was that it had to do with some long-ago scandal revolving around the family's money having been lost by a dissolute ancestor. Too bloody long ago to be of any consequence, if you ask me. So, in answer to your question, my darling wife, my roots have bugger all to do with it.'

Beth had skipped dessert in favour of coffee. The offer had come out of the blue and she was totally unprepared. She could tell Martin was keen on the idea but she had her reservations. She hesitated a moment before saying, 'I don't know, Martin. It's a huge step. When we've talked in the past about moving out of London to somewhere more rural, I'd imagined somewhere in the south. Sussex maybe, or Berkshire, or even Hampshire. Durham is just so far away. And isn't it supposed to be cold up there? It's almost Scotland.'

'Probably a tad colder, I suppose. By a few degrees possibly but, never having been further north than Manchester, I'm afraid I can't say.'

Beth didn't remind him that when he'd returned from Manchester, he'd said that he'd found it bloody cold and wet and was glad to be back home.

He leaned over the table and took hold of her hand. 'Beth, darling, it's a really fantastic opportunity. My own branch. Free rein as far as staffing is concerned. Who knows? If I can make a real go of it, more northeast branches could follow, which undoubtedly would lead to another step up the ladder, and consequently a lot more money. Not to be sniffed at, if you ask me.'

Martin could see she was yet to be convinced, so he continued. 'Think of what they're offering. A thirty percent pay rise, company car, relocation expenses, plus generous commission depending on the success of the venture.' He signalled to a passing waiter and ordered himself a coffee. 'And another thing,' he went on, obviously hoping that what he would say next would further his cause, 'with the money we'll walk away with from the sale of the house here, we'd be able to afford something much more substantial. Maybe even consider a self-build. Incorporate a studio where you would have the luxury of working from home. We've always fancied that. Building a house to our own specifications.'

Beth gave him that look he'd become only too familiar with over the years.

'OK, to *your* specifications.'

They grinned at each other. Still in love. After more than six years together, Beth and Martin had grown to know each other's tastes. Their quirks. Their shortfalls.

'It would definitely need to be to *my* specifications, absolutely and exclusively,' Beth teased. 'You might be Mr Super Salesman, my love, but great taste, or practicality for that matter, are most decidedly lacking, as you readily admit.'

'Ah, but I have great taste in women,' Martin countered.

'This is true,' Beth quipped. 'So, how long have they given you to decide?'

'Gerry's asked me to think it through over the weekend and get back to him by Monday lunch time.' He paused for a moment before adding, 'Beth, if I turn this down, they might never again consider me as a candidate to run my own branch. Anyway, I suspect their second option would be to offer the job to that prick, Brian Jessop. I'm not sure I could put up with his gloating, even for the short time before he takes up the post.'

Beth couldn't believe he'd been given so little time to reach what amounted to a life-changing decision. She could understand Martin's enthusiasm but it didn't stop her from having doubts. She needed time to think it through. 'Let me sleep on it,' she conceded, 'and do some checking. I need to consider what it is I might be subjecting myself to if we move to the wild and windy north.'

Martin Wilshaw desperately wanted to take up the offer, but he also desperately didn't want to have a row with Beth. He watched her now as she left the table and walked towards the ladies, her mountain of curly black hair in beautiful disarray as usual. She claimed she'd given up the quest for the elusive stylist that could tame the unruly mass, so she'd decided to let it grow. Let it do its own thing. Today, as on most days, she'd piled it up into some sort of untidy knot. He still couldn't believe his luck. Time had done nothing to lessen his desire. He decided he'd better not push her too hard for the moment. And anyway, she'd said she'd think about it. He'd leave it at that for the time being. Besides, it was a foregone conclusion that he'd get his way. He invariably did. He'd just have to be patient. He watched her as she returned to the table and, once she'd sat down, risked one more comment in his attempt to win her over.

'Imagine what you could do with a self-build. Your own studio designed to your own specifications. No more working in that poky box room.'

Beth's bespoke online jewellery business was finally beginning to flourish and she had begun to make a bit of a name for herself.

'I said I'd think about it, Martin,' she said, 'and I will.' Beth smiled to lessen the impact of her initial lack of enthusiasm, seeing his obvious disappointment. 'Can we please drop the subject for the time being and enjoy the rest of the day? It's a big ask to be suddenly confronted with. Surely you had some sort of inkling that the offer was in the pipeline?'

'I thought it wise not to presume.'

No more was said on the subject of the possible move north as they ambled arm-in-arm along the towpath to their pretty two-storey mid-terrace home in Putney.

And nor was it discussed the following Sunday morning. Beth could see that as the day progressed, although he refrained from mentioning the subject, Martin was becoming agitated, waiting for her decision.

It puzzled her that her husband had proved himself to be so successful in the estate agency business. She'd always thought it was the aggressive, go-getting, ruthless types who shot up the ladder in that particular business. Maybe he was different in the workplace. More assertive with staff and colleagues than he was at home. Perhaps she'd been misreading him all these years and he actually *was* the go-getting type. Or maybe his success simply stemmed from hard work and, of course, that aura of trustworthiness that had drawn her to him in the first place. He seemed to have the knack of persuading sellers and buyers alike that they were dealing with a knowledgeable and honest estate agent who would tell them how it was rather than what they wanted to hear. Whatever the reason, he had proved himself to be excellent at his chosen career, as demonstrated by the current situation.

After the substantial Sunday lunch, and a little too much wine, they settled down together on the sofa. Beth put her head on Martin's shoulder and said, 'I know you're dying to ask but please don't. I'm still looking into it, but I promise you'll have my answer by tomorrow morning.'

Great, thought Martin, *another sleepless night.*

But that wasn't to be the case. Beth took herself off to her little cramped box room, citing work as an excuse. Later, as the couple took their Sunday evening stroll, Beth put him out of his misery.

'It's quite exciting, isn't it?' she said.

'What is?'

'All that history. The cathedral, the castle, Beamish Museum, Hamsterley Forest, the Bowes Museum, Crook Hall. I've been doing some research. So much more culture than I imagined. And that's without the nearby delights of Northumberland and the north-east coast.' She knew she was teasing him. She grabbed Martin's hand. 'Okay, worry guts, let's do it.'

'You're sure?

'I'm sure.'

Martin picked her up, swung her around and smacked a great big kiss on her lips before setting her back on her feet.

'I have told you, have I not, Mrs Wilshaw, that I love you, wholeheartedly, absolutely and unconditionally?' 'Many times, Mr Wilshaw, many times.'

***

It all happened remarkably quickly once the decision was made. The house went on the market, and as they'd expected, with Putney being such a sought-after area of west London, it was snapped up almost immediately, and at a premium price. After a few weekend visits to Durham, Martin found a small rental property in the centre of the city that he would initially occupy alone while Beth stayed south to temporarily suspend her business, pack up the house and arrange for the majority of the contents to be put into storage for the time being.

When Martin took up his new post in mid-March, the blossom was heavy on the trees in London, but had yet to appear in Durham. The new owners of the Putney property took possession in early May, which is when Beth joined Martin, happily experiencing the emergence of spring for a second time. As anticipated, house prices in the Durham area proved to be substantially lower than those in Putney. The couple excitedly calculated that they now really were in a position to consider a self-build, if they could find suitable land. Any initial doubts that Beth had harboured about building a new life away from the bustle of the capital were cast aside within days of her arrival in Durham. She had fallen in love with the city from the very first visit. Life was exciting. Full of promise.

***

A few weeks into the search, Beth was out shopping in Durham city centre when her mobile rang. Expecting a call from her sister, Chris, Beth was surprised to see that the caller was Martin. It was still over an hour away before their agreed get-together to grab a quick lunch.

'Hi, darling,' he said, 'where are you?'

'Shopping in the city centre. What's up?'

'Listen, Beth, I think I might have found the perfect place for the build. We've only just taken instructions on it this morning so it's not yet on the open market. I think it could be ideal.'

'Go on,' Beth prompted, excitement mounting.

'It's a couple of acres of disused land on the outskirts of a pretty village called Lanchester. Only a fifteen-to-twenty-minute drive from Durham. Perfect for a quick commute to work. Apparently, there's a dilapidated old stone cottage on the site which, from what I've been told, wouldn't take much to demolish.'

'And you couldn't wait until lunch to tell me? It must be something pretty special.'

'Oh, I think it is. Which is why I'm ringing you now in case you have plans for the afternoon and, if so, can you cancel? I've agreed to view the property straight after lunch so thought we could go together. Check it out.'

'You mean you'd like me to cancel my hairdo, my manicure, pedicure, facial, and a quickie with my latest lover to look at some fields?'

'Exactly!'

'Okay then. See you soon.' Beth ended the call, stood for a moment before making for a vacant bench in the market square. She'd recently been rethinking the plan to self-build. The trouble was, having lived in such close proximity to the city centre for the several weeks she'd been here, she was beginning to lose the urge to move to a rural setting, especially as they'd viewed some rather beautiful properties on the immediate outskirts of the city. But Martin's enthusiasm during his call being so evident, Beth decided she ought to defer judgment until after the afternoon's viewing.

As they drove up to the site, they were immediately struck not only by the prettiness of the neat little village, but by the beauty of the surrounding landscape. The property, as far as they could tell at first glance, was situated on a gentle rolling hill with views east down into the village centre, overlooking the twelfth century All Saints church. To the west was an uninterrupted and spectacular view of the edge of the moors which Beth knew led on to the hills of the north Pennines. The road running along the south boundary to the property was defined by an ancient hedgerow, now seriously overgrown. Beth recognised hawthorn intermingled with bramble and possibly blackberry. That was as far as her knowledge went on the subject of hedges, but she mentally patted herself on the back for the fact that she'd managed to identify as much as she did. The rest of the site was defined by a dry-stone wall, collapsed in places, but nonetheless beautiful in Beth's opinion. She ran her hand over the stones, feeling the warmth of moss and lichen.

'First impressions?' asked Martin.

'I'm reserving judgment for the moment,' Beth lied, wanting Martin to believe the ultimate decision would lie with him. Chris would have accused her of pandering to his ego. In truth, Beth was already smitten. She hadn't ever considered herself to have been an impulsive person, but for whatever reason, she realised she'd made an instant decision. She knew she already belonged. *Crazy*, she thought, *but nevertheless, true.*

Chapter Two

Ah, she's arrived, me bonnie. Me perfectly formed, raven-haired bonnie. She's perfect, Pickie. Can you tell she's mine? Can you tell from her beautiful hair? Her bonnie face? Nobody ever told me I was bonnie. Not bonnie like the ladies that came to Hill House. I was flawed. Misshapen. That's what folk said about me. As though that was the only thing they noticed about me. As though that one thing defined me. 'That young Bessie Ellis's flawed. Born that way. A cripple. Not properly made.' Like it was my fault. Anyhow, a misshapen foot didn't mean me mind was flawed. And, see, me bonnie's not flawed. Nobody could deny me beautiful hair though. I had really beautiful hair, just like her, didn't I, Pickie? And nice straight teeth. Mebbe I'd've been considered bonnie if I'd been born to a ma and da who loved me and took care of me. Or born into privilege instead of that hovel me da called a farm. Two measly fields, a dozen or so sheep and scrawny chickens peckin' and shittin' all over the yard. Anyway, bein' considered bonnie wouldn't've done me any good, would it, Pickie? More than likely would've made things even worse.

Chapter Three

'Let's explore,' Beth said as she moved ahead of Martin, eager to find the derelict building that had been mentioned.

'Can't see any derelict building so far,' she commented as they strolled along what had obviously once been a track, now only just discernible under a covering of weeds and moss.

'Apparently it's just on the other side of that slight incline,' answered Martin.

Reaching the top of the slope, they came across it.

Martin looked at what was left of the building. 'No wonder we couldn't see it. Not so much a building as a pile of rubble,' he commented.

The only evidence that it had once been a dwelling was a waist-high, south-facing stone wall abutting what would have been the wall to the east, but which was now just an assortment of boulders and rocks of varying sizes.

Pointing to the north where, about twenty metres down from the derelict building stood an imposing lone tree, Beth nudged Martin. 'That's a pretty magnificent looking specimen. Any idea what sort of tree it is?'

They both strolled over to inspect it.

'Haven't a fucking clue,' he replied.

'You disappoint me.'

'Easy enough to find out,' said Martin, taking out his phone and googling British trees. After less than a minute he had the answer. 'Looks to me as though it might be a yew. What do you reckon?'

Beth leant over and checked the picture on the phone.

'Think you're right,' she said. 'It must be pretty ancient given the size of it. I think it's rather spectacular, standing there alone in all its glory.'

'I'm not really into trees so can't comment one way or the other,' Martin said, dismissively. They turned and wandered back to the remains of the farmhouse or cottage, whatever it had been once upon a time.

The building had been situated in what seemed to be the approximate centre of the field. They stood and gazed out over the land, taking in the extent of the property.

'Been pretty much neglected over the years,' commented Martin.

'A blinking great meadow,' said Beth, adding, 'with lots of potential.'

'For what?' asked Martin.

'Oh, I don't know. Growing things? Keeping chickens? Rearing pigs?'

'Not pigs,' groaned Martin. 'You can't be serious. Never, ever will I live within sight or sound of grunting, smelly pigs, even if they're the things you desire more than anything else in the world.'

Beth feigned a sad sigh. 'Ah, you just don't love me enough,' she said, moving off to explore what would have been the interior of the once-standing building. Stepping through a gap in the rubble, to what was once the inside of the building, but where any floor was obscured by grass and weed, Beth was immediately drawn to what she determined must have been the rear of the property, facing west. She instantly knew that this was where the kitchen, the main hub of the house, had once stood. There was no evidence for this. She simply knew. And there was an odd certainty to the knowledge that she couldn't explain. It was then, standing there, that she experienced an overwhelming sense of déjà vu. The feeling was so strong that she decided there and then that, whatever Martin thought, this was where they would make their home. That her workshop would be constructed on the very spot on which she was standing. It was where she felt an almost uncanny and inexplicable need to be.

Martin came and stood behind Beth, folding his arms around her waist. 'What do you think, darling?'

'I'm beginning to think it's perfect,' Beth said leaning into him. 'What about you?'

He surprised her by hesitating. 'I don't know. Now that I'm here I'm having reservations. It initially seemed like the ideal location; the space, the views, the locality. But for some reason my enthusiasm seems to be waning a bit. And I can't put my finger on why that should be.'

'Scared of the amount of the work involved?'

29

'Of course not. That's not it. Anyway, you'd be the one doing the work. We always knew it would be your own personal project, me being, as you so often remind me, cack-handed, impractical and devoid of any style or aesthetic sense, whatever that is. Anyway, not scared exactly, but I do admit to an inexplicable feeling of apprehension.'

'Weird, Martin. So unlike you. It strikes me as being the ideal place. Look at the views. As you said yourself, it's no more than a fifteen-minute drive to Durham city centre, and it's within walking distance of that gorgeous little village, albeit a twenty or so minute walk, so it's not entirely remote. That's a plus in my book, along with all the other pluses I can see.'

'I think we should sleep on it before diving in headlong. Agreed?'

'Fair comment. But try not to dither for too long. I have to warn you that I'm already envisioning our dream home.'

Chapter Four

Me da was the first. The filthy bugger. Ah, aye, he broke me in all right. And Ma didn't do nothin.' Always bein' told you're a good-for-nothin' cripple makes you do as you're told. I was supposed to be grateful. For what, Pickie? The only thing I'm grateful for is that our tree rested us in her arms until she found them. Our day is almost come, Pickie. She's let us know what needs doin' and we'll soon be at work. Good work. Necessary work. Healin' work.

Chapter Five

After a couple of days of discussion, a second visit to Lanchester, lots of persuasion on Beth's part, and against his better judgment, Martin finally capitulated. He was used to having his own way when it came to Beth, but in this case, she was unusually determined. He had to remind himself that he'd promised she'd have the final say in what he'd said would be her own personal project.

Martin's training in his chosen industry wouldn't allow him to pay the asking price and, after lots of negotiation, and much to Beth's relief, a reduced offer was accepted. Beth immediately set to work on ideas for her dream home, sketching the layout and imagining the end result. Later, in retrospect, she remembered how ecstatically happy and excited she'd been during those early days.

***

While Martin spent the majority of his time setting up the new agency, researching the local market and recruiting staff, Beth worked closely with her chosen architect. James Douglas, an associate of one of the larger and well-respected practices in the area. His had been the first company she'd visited and she had engaged his services without consulting any other firm. When she'd shyly presented him with her rough sketches of the proposed building, Beth had expected to be faced with a number of objections or criticisms, or the unviability of the design. But James had congratulated her on her excellent vision. There would, he explained, of necessity, be some adjustments and compromises to be made but, overall, he considered Beth's ideas workable and, what's more, he called them visionary and impressive. Beth had been flattered. And, more by luck than judgment, James turned out to be an excellent choice.

He and Beth worked well together. From start to finish they rarely disagreed. The one thing he did try to dissuade her from was where her workshop should be situated, which she insisted was to be on the ground floor, exactly where she'd been certain the original kitchen had stood, and to where she'd been inexplicably drawn since that very first visit. James didn't like the idea, suggesting that the space would be better suited to some sort of utility and storage area. But Beth stood her ground, and when she pointed out her intention to install a wall of glass, he finally agreed.

Early on, he'd realised the futility of arguing his point too strongly when it came to Beth's plans for her workshop. She was happy to capitulate on his suggestions for other areas but she was adamant on her plans for her studio and workshop. It was decided that a small kitchen area as well as an en-suite would be installed to save unnecessary trips upstairs whilst working. The main living area was to be on the first floor, with a wide balcony running around three sides, accessed through a number of folding glass doors in order to maximise the view.

She hoped the height of the building would enable a view of the distant moors, behind which, she knew from her research, rose the hills of the North Pennines. In those early spring days Beth could only imagine the spectacular colour of the heather in bloom. She'd already noticed, at the side of the road leading up to the site, that the gorse was just about to start producing its bright yellow blossom.

***

As the weeks went by and Beth spent more and more time studying the plans, overseeing the construction along with James, the pair making mutually agreed adjustments, Martin had been spending more and more time building his team, finalising the fitting out of the office, and he was now concentrating his efforts on seeking clients. It became the norm for the couple to meet up a couple of times a week to have lunch and to chat with Martin's new colleagues. Beth had immediately warmed to the secretary or office administrator, Bridget, a no-nonsense but kindly, mature woman in her fifties.

In addition; there were three negotiators, Malcolm was an enthusiastic twenty-something local boy with a broad accent who happily explained he was the junior learning on the job. Beth was taken with his open smile and almost humble demeanour on being presented with 'the boss's wife'. Harold was a tall thick-set man in his early fifties who Martin had admitted he'd shamelessly recruited from a competitor. On their first encounter, Beth recalled experiencing an unpleasant although momentary sensation, almost like she imagined an electric shock might feel, as he took her extended hand in both of his and looked much too intently into her eyes, saying how delightful it was to meet at last. The feeling, which Beth could only describe to herself as being one of revulsion, passed when Harold reluctantly, it seemed, released her hand. Beth was at a loss to work out what had just happened. As Harold moved back to his desk, she couldn't stop herself from wiping her hand on the side of her trousers, hoping no one noticed.

And then there was Fiona. Beth rarely made assumptions about people she'd only just met but there was something about Fiona that rankled. It might have been the coldness of the greeting when Fiona briefly gave a dismissive nod in Beth's direction before turning and walking away, her curvy figure sheathed in an over-tight pencil skirt, and long legs ending in impossibly high designer shoes. Or maybe it was the bleached, expertly cut bob, mascaraed lashes and pouting rouged lips. Beth couldn't help but feel uncomfortable at what she perceived as her own lack of style, before mentally berating herself for her too quick, and more than likely, unfair judgment. After all, she didn't know the woman. Nevertheless, it seemed apparent that Fiona, who Beth guessed was around her own age, was more interested in herself than in other people. And Beth couldn't help but find Fiona intimidating. Glancing again at the sharp haircut, Beth was reminded of her own unruly locks and minimum make-up. She also couldn't help but notice how Fiona put her hand on Martin's arm when seeking his attention. The action seemed overly familiar. Beth's initial assessment, despite her earlier remorse for jumping to conclusions, was further compounded by the way Fiona talked down to young Malcolm, upbraiding him loudly and sternly regarding figures which she said should have been on her desk yesterday. Telling him that he needed to buck up his ideas. Surely, Beth thought, it would have been courteous to wait until she'd left, or to at least have taken the boy to one side out of the earshot of others. Later, when Beth voiced her concerns to Martin he shrugged it off, explaining that Fiona was already proving to be a valuable asset, bringing in even more business than Harold from the word go. If that meant they all had to put up with a bit of discomfort from her superior attitude in the short term, he was confident it would pay off. He assured Beth that Fiona would eventually learn that he wouldn't tolerate bullying.

Chapter Six

It pains me to see me bonnie in the company of that connivin' no-good Gregory, curse him and all his kin. How could I not recognise those deceitful mollycoddled features? The feigned warmth in those coppery eyes with the pale lashes. The same lank fair hair. They have to pay, Pickie. Denied me rest they did, even as I lived. That last one made a mistake when he rested us where he did. Givin' us into the arms of the yew where she holds us yet. But she's waked us. Rewarded us for our patience. Our loving keeper will have her feast at the end of it all.

Chapter Seven

Harold hadn't divulged his real reason for moving on from his previous job. Neither had he said anything about his current abysmal living conditions. Admittedly he'd pushed her too far in the end. She'd always forgiven him in the past. Every time she found out, that is. Not after the last one though. Debbie had been the last straw as far as she was concerned. He'd always had a thing for petite, dark haired women and there were just too many of them about. And where had it got him in the end? In a fucking shared house with housemates who seemed to think that living in squalor was acceptible. He'd have to look for an alternative before he caught something untreatable from the filth. He'd never considered himself a stickler for cleanliness, but their disgusting lack of hygiene went beyond the pale. And there was his wife and kid shacked up nicely with that bastard, Terry bloody Page, in his four-bed detached, being topped up monthly with maintenance payments that were crippling him. Some fucking boss Terry had turned out to be when the chips were down.

And now, even little Debbie had told him where to go. Marry her? Why the fuck would he even begin to think about ever getting married again?

Mind you, he hadn't expected Martin's wife to be so attractive. More than that. She was the sort of woman he had always envisaged as his ideal. For Christ's sake, he told himself, keep yourself in check, you randy sod. After the last fiasco, the last thing he needed was to make an idiot of himself. Anyway, how could he even consider that a young thing like her could possibly be tempted by an old bugger like him. Hopefully he'd get lucky down at the club this weekend.

***

Martin rarely agreed to Beth's requests for him to accompany her to check out the progress the builders were making on the house, giving the excuse of either being too tied up with work, or, in the evenings, claiming to be too tired to tramp around a muddy building site. The truth was, he felt he'd made a big mistake. He should have insisted on checking out other places before diving in. But Beth had been unusually insistent and he'd finally given in. After all, he'd promised it would be her project. He didn't know why the place made him feel so fucking uncomfortable but he just knew it did. He didn't like being there. There was something about the place that unsettled him. But it was too bloody late now. Beth, quite reasonably, he admitted to himself, couldn't understand his reluctance to accompany her to the site, but had accepted his assertion that it was only because he wanted the end result to surprise him. That he trusted her completely until that time. He placated Beth by spending the weekends browsing with her through brochures of kitchen fittings, white goods, bathrooms, as well as accompanying her to furniture outlets and builders' merchants. Whatever she decided on, he agreed to.

'Being given free rein on every decision is one thing, Martin, but your total disinterest is beginning to irritate,' she'd said to him one Saturday afternoon in the soft furnishing department of John Lewis.

'Beth, darling, you know I have complete faith in you,' he said. 'For the time being it's essential for me to concentrate on making money and ensuring the new set-up is attracting good solid business. It won't always be like this, I promise.' Martin put his arm around Beth's shoulder, kissed her on the cheek and said, 'Tell you what, tomorrow we'll go there together and I'll be more than happy to admire the progress and to listen while you explain what goes where, how the space will work, and talk till your heart's content about how wonderful our life will be. Then, my clever, talented wife, we'll have a bloody huge slap-up lunch, drink expensive wine and maybe, or rather hopefully, spend the rest of the day and night in bed doing what we do best. What say you?'

Beth was instantly cheered, kissed him back and said, 'Sounds like a plan.'

At this late stage, Martin couldn't possibly confess to the ridiculous and inexplicable feeling that overcame him by just setting foot on the site. He had to keep telling himself he was being absurdly fanciful. It wasn't in his nature to be superstitious, and yet he couldn't help himself. He repeatedly put the feeling down to having been working too hard, believing that any doubts he had would disappear once the house was finished and they finally moved in.

***

Malcolm thought life would be perfect if it wasn't for Fiona. He was learning a lot. His dad had been right to put him off going to university. 'Learn on the job, son,' he'd said, 'not like those other poor sods coming out of uni with nothing but a load of debt hanging round their necks.' Malcolm had worked hard to achieve decent A level results and was now sailing through the estate agent exams. In a few months he'd be out on the road on his own evaluating properties, and when that happened his income would go up and he might even be able to think of buying a little place of his own. Not that he didn't like living at home, but he couldn't live there forever. One day he hoped he'd be able to knock the high and mighty Fiona off her perch. But that was a long way off. For the time being he just had to put up with her. Dad had said, 'There's always one, son. Always one awkward bugger wherever you go. Just get on with the job and don't let her get to you.' And that's what Malcolm intended to do, especially as everybody else in the office was easy to get on with. Harold was a bit grumpy sometimes but he always apologised afterwards.

***

Beth was feeling upbeat on Sunday morning, with Martin seeming enthusiastic about checking out the progress. Arriving at the site, she could see that he was definitely impressed by how much had been achieved since his last visit. The house was really beginning to take shape. The walls were up and the rafters were in place, although the roof was as yet a little way from the tiling stage, the interior being protected by a layer of plastic sheeting. And the double garage was completely finished. Beth realised that, until then, Martin hadn't been able to envisage how impressive the building was going to look when finished, especially now that the reclaimed, double-width oak doors were in situ. 'Nice and wide for our wheelchairs when we're old and frail,' she joked.

Once inside, Beth went about explaining the layout. The central staircase led up from the substantial hall and split into two on the first-floor landing, the right hand leading to the huge main double-aspect living area and then on through to the large kitchen, while to the left would be the master suite plus two further bedrooms and a bathroom. As she'd explained to him before, both the living areas and the master suite were to have wall-to-wall, ceiling to floor, glazed folding doors to take advantage of the view.

'Impressed?' Beth asked.

'Spectacular!' Martin replied. And she could see he meant it. She knew that with the invaluable help of James Douglas she had managed to create something really special. Despite the confidence she felt, Beth was both relieved and appreciative of Martin's praise. But then he disappointed her when his next comment was, 'It's so amazing, Beth, that I can't help wondering what it would bring were we to put it straight back on the market once it's finished.'

'Well, that's not going to happen!' Beth said, glaring at him. Martin immediately realised he'd said the wrong thing.

'Just joking,' he laughed, taking her hand as they went back down the stairs.

Beth was keen to show him her studio which, like the garage, was almost finished.

'I'm really excited about this, Martin. My very own on-site studio. I can't wait to get it fitted out. I imagine I'll be spending a lot of time in here.'

On entering the studio, Martin experienced the same sense of unease he'd had before. *It's weird*, he thought. *Like that first time, it's this particular area that gives me the bloody creeps*. He stood just inside the doorway, not willing to enter the space and wanting Beth to be back at his side. Beth beckoned him over, intending to show him where her work table would be situated so she'd be able to take in the view from the huge windows and the lone yew tree as she worked, and to demonstrate how she'd be able to take advantage of the light when crafting her pieces. Martin tried to look enthusiastic but didn't approach, simply agreeing that he could see from where he was standing that it would be an excellent place to work. He didn't like this room, but how could he explain? Instead, as a diversion, he looked pointedly at his watch and said they'd have to leave now if they were to get a table at The Mill and, as far as he was concerned, he'd said nothing that could have brought on what happened next.

Beth was suddenly overcome with rage. 'Why are you always so bloody reluctant to even try to show some interest?' she screamed at him, unable to hold back her fury. 'I have to practically beg you to come and look at what will be our home and when you do deign to *humour* me you can't get away quickly enough.'

The ferocity of her rage wasn't only unexpected but, as far as Martin was concerned, completely unwarranted, and not at all what he'd come to expect from Beth. It was so out of character that it shocked him. Never before had he known her to lose her temper so completely. Still fuming, Beth stormed past him, violently shoving him aside as she made for the door, causing him to knock his elbow painfully against the frame.

'Fuck!' he shouted. 'That was my fucking funny bone. What the hell's got into you?'

Once outside Beth seemed to come to her senses. She began to calm down. She couldn't recall ever before experiencing such deep anger, and the level of hostility she felt towards Martin, just for those few moments, had really scared her. It was like she'd morphed into somebody she didn't recognise. Realising what she'd done, she turned to see Martin still standing in the doorway with a look of astonishment and utter confusion on his face.

'Oh God, Martin, I'm so sorry,' she said, and meant it. 'Honestly, I don't know what got into me. Banging your funny bone isn't funny, is it! Is it really painful?'

Martin was holding his elbow and scowling at her. Beth tentatively approached intending to put her arms around him, again telling him how sorry she was. He simply nodded, shrugged her off and made for the car.

They were both unnaturally quiet during the drive back to Durham, and the subject of Beth's sudden and unexpected outburst was dropped. But each of them was reliving the incident with growing incredulity.

Martin parked the car at the flat and they strolled to the restaurant. On the way he reached for Beth's hand and, with a great sense of relief, Beth took it. It seemed all would be well.

Chapter Eight

There was no happiness in me short life. And that matters, Pickie. It matters a lot. Me life was filled with nowt but misery from the start. Things got a bit better when I was sent to Hill House, I suppose. Anywhere away from me ma and da was better. But it was only better for a short while, and only because of me "gift". At least that's what the mistress said I had when she put me full-time to the needle. A gift! That's what she'd called it. Of course, that was after eighteen months of scrubbin' and mendin' in the hot, steamy laundry before the mistress even knew I existed. If it hadn't been for Mrs Bull I might've stayed there, slavin' away, hands raw, even blisterin' and bleedin.' At first it was the stitchin' of the hems on the sheets where they'd frayed, then to darnin' the petticoats. Mrs Bull said I had a neatness of hand and a fine eye. She showed me how to redo the bits that'd come adrift from the embroidered initials on the napkins, which I admit I enjoyed. I was proud of meself, Pickie. I wanted to learn more. I wanted to make beautiful things. Mrs Bull was really kind. She let me practise on bits of scrap. If only she hadn't brought me work to the attention of the mistress, I think I would've been happy to spend me days sewin' in the laundry, even though I suffered at first from sore fingertips. But they soon toughened up. Lookin' back, I think that was the only time in me whole life that I was content. Sittin' on the stool in the corner of the steamy laundry workin' on the linen. And the best thing about workin' at Hill House was that I was only allowed home for a half day on Sundays. Bloody Sundays! I'd've rather carried on workin'. The mistress thought she was doin' me a favour givin' me the time off. Orderin' me to spend it visiting me ma and da, as if I had any choice. Some bloody favour! Havin' to traipse all the way there and back only to hand over all but tuppence of me measly wages to the bastard and me miserable excuse for a ma. Me ma, who'd turned a blind eye. But I couldn't turn a blind eye to her growing belly, could I? Mebbe I shouldn't have blamed her for not lookin' out for me, havin' witnessed the beatin's she'd put up with over the years. But I did. I blamed her, Pickie. And I do still. More than ever.

Chapter Nine

For weeks Beth had been hoping that Christine would get the chance to visit. Despite being the younger by three years, Chris had always been the strong sister. The one Beth leant on. Relied upon for her practicality and good sense. Beth knew that Chris's work in public relations kept her busy, especially as the company had been going through a boom time, but Chris had promised that, once things calmed down a bit, she'd be up like a shot. They talked at least twice a week on the phone but Beth missed her sister's physical presence. Now, finally, Chris had managed to organise a long weekend. She would arrive on Friday evening and leave Monday morning. Beth couldn't wait to show her the build which, thanks to James's excellent connections in the trade, and the weather having been kind, was now getting very close to completion. The electricians and plumbers had almost finished, which meant that the flooring and tiling could be started the following week. Then would come the stage that Beth was looking forward to the most — the choosing of the furnishings and all those lovely finishing touches which would turn their house into a home.

Beth met Chris off the train at seven thirty, on a warm September evening. True to form, after the usual hugs, Chris said, 'Right, little big sister, where's the nearest pub?' She looked around before adding, 'And where's the bloody car?'

'No car. No need,' Beth answered, still hugging her. 'We're walking. And before you complain, I promise you it's a very short walk.'

'What about this overstuffed backpack? You mean I've got to do a pub crawl lugging the thing around all night?'

'Of course not,' Beth laughed. 'That's Martin's job.'

Within minutes they were in Martin's office where he was just finishing up. Greetings and kisses exchanged, Martin took charge of the bag and they strolled along to The Head of Steam, finding a recently vacated table in the courtyard.

'A few good real ales on tap here, Chris,' Martin said.

'Ah, you know me so well, you lovely man. I'll have what you're having, and make it a pint.'

'You think I'd dare to bring you a half?' Martin joked.

Martin and Chris had hit it off from their very first meeting, for which Beth was thankful. She didn't know what she'd have done had it been otherwise. She could never imagine being in the position of having to choose between the two.

As the evening wore on the banter between Martin and Chris flowed as usual.

'Can't wait to see this spectacular new house that your wife has been going on and on and bloody on about like a broken record,' Chris said, grinning at Beth.

'Well,' Beth piped up, 'you'll have to wait until Sunday because tomorrow you and I are going shopping.'

'And a bit of celebratory drinking, I hope? It's what weekends are for.'

'Not until you've given an opinion on some soft furnishings I've got in mind. In my experience, your judgment becomes excessively clouded with daytime drinking and you'll persuade me to go for the exact opposite of what I envisage.'

Chris rolled her eyes at Martin. 'I expect I'll be confronted with an array of tasteful and expensive fabrics which she knows I'll disapprove of, my preference, as you both well know, being for the gaudy. My sister is far too conservative in her taste, don't you think, Martin?'

Martin cast his eye meaningfully over Chris, taking in the bleached white-blonde, close-cropped hair, nose stud, skin-tight off-the-shoulder black top — designed, no doubt, to reveal the shoulder tattoo — floaty wide-bottomed pants and a multi-coloured fringed silk shawl, the whole ensemble finished off with an excessive number of beaded necklaces to match the long dangling earrings. To his mind her appearance seemed to hover somewhere between punk and gipsy fortune-teller.

'No,' he answered, deadpan.

Their friendly repartee was a constant source of both relief and delight to Beth and much later, on looking back, she remembered how happy she'd been on that particular evening.

People who didn't know Beth and Chris wouldn't take them for sisters, they being so dissimilar. But the sisters felt that they were closer than many birth siblings. They had often found themselves explaining how they were adopted three years apart. Chris was taller than Beth by several inches, and the difference didn't stop there. Chris tended to be flamboyant and outgoing. On first meeting, her overly confident demeanour had struck some as a tendency to be bossy, whereas Beth recognised it for what it was, Chris' determination to look after her more reserved sister. Chris considered Beth to be a bit of a shrinking violet and, in comparison to Chris's outgoing and bubbly personality, Beth accepted this assessment as understandable. And, she supposed, it was true, after all.

***

The weather on Sunday morning was disappointingly dull and quite chilly so Beth wore a sweater over her top and also provided one for Chris who, despite the size of her backpack, hadn't brought one, simply, she said, because it was summer. 'Summers are supposed to be warm,' she moaned.

'A few degrees lower than London is more than compensated for by the freshness of the air, the beauty of the landscape, the open spaces, etcetera,' Martin teased, aware of the hangover Chris must be suffering from after the over-indulgence of the previous evening.

'I'm unaccustomed to the cold, I'll have you know, Martin. Why the bloody hell couldn't you have got a job somewhere warm and sunny, like Spain or Greece? Or even anywhere south of Luton?' moaned Chris, looking sorry for herself.

Having admired the pretty village as they drove through, and then arriving at the site, Chris perked up and gave a loud 'Wow!' adding, 'This looks absolutely amazing!'

'All down to your talented sister,' said Martin, grabbing each of them by the elbow and shunting them towards the front door.

'It's really something,' said Chris, 'and what absolutely stunning views. Can't wait to see the inside.'

Entering through the big oak door, they made their way up to the first floor where Beth revelled in Chris's effusive compliments.

'It's absolutely amazing, sis,' she said, gazing out over the landscape and putting her arm around Beth's shoulder. 'I'm really, really proud of you. What an achievement! How did you get to be so talented while I have to earn my living slaving away in a boring old office?'

'Ah, but you make stacks of money working in a boring old office, while I bugger about making a pittance and divesting my indulgent husband of his hard-earned money.'

'You're such a pushover,' Chris said to Martin, poking him playfully in the ribs. 'Right, can we please bloody go now that I've expressed my undying admiration for what will become your new abode. I'm desperate to get into the warmth, and even more desperate for a large glass of something warming to take the chill off my bones.'

'Just one more room to admire,' said Beth, leading the way down the stairs.

Chapter Ten

She knew this room, Pickie. Knew it as soon as she arrived. She knows it's where she needs to be. I've been given another gift now. I wasn't rested here all this time without heedin' our tree. She put this gift in me. The proof of it lies in me bonnie's drawin' to this very place. Because it wasn't her that was drawn to it. It was me that drew her. Our tree blessed me with this gift. She made me part of her. Give me the power of the lodestone. The gift of drawin'.

Chapter Eleven

'And this,' declared Beth, 'is my wonderful new studio.' She moved to the window to indicate where her workbench would be.'

Martin, as he had the last time, remained in the doorway while Chris walked over to where her sister was standing. As she did so, a shiver ran through Martin.

Chris was less impressed with the studio than she had been with the rest of the building. 'Hm,' she said, 'it's a bit small. Good view though.'

'Plenty big enough for my purposes,' countered Beth, 'and there's loads of storage space in the garage next door if I need it. How much space do you need to make jewellery! You know, Chris, even on my first visit to the site, I felt this was where I needed to be. Exactly here, in this spot. Isn't that strange?'

'You're just weird,' said Chris, putting her arm around Beth.

'Just look at the view, Chris, then tell me whether or not I'm weird. It's inspirational.'

Chris moved closer to the huge glass windows, and in doing so, her eyes were drawn to the lone tree.

'That's a pretty impressive looking tree,' she said. 'Looks ancient.'

'It's a yew,' piped up Martin from the doorway. 'Apparently, they can live for centuries. Possibly the longest living of all trees native to Europe.'

'Impressive,' Chris commented. 'Now, can we get going, before I die of thirst?'

The chill of the morning having been replaced by glorious sunshine, once outside, Chris and Beth removed their sweaters before getting into the car.

'How did you get that bruise on your arm?' Chris asked.

'What bruise?' Beth said, looking at her forearms. 'Oh! No idea. Didn't notice it this morning. Must have accidentally knocked myself somehow. Didn't feel it though.'

'She's tougher than she looks,' said Martin. 'Where do you fancy for lunch?'

The bruise was forgotten.

***

A couple of weeks after Chris's visit, the house, subject to some minor snagging, was more or less finished and Martin and Beth moved in at the beginning of October. The weather, although well into autumn, was still reasonably warm after a mild September. Wanting to take time to settle in, they decided to postpone their planned house-warming celebration until the end of the month, intending to keep it small, inviting only Martin's work colleagues, James the architect, and, of course, Chris, if she could make it. Beth had been so tied up with the planning, construction and furnishing of the house that she now regretted having not made the time to forge friendships, or even acquaintances, either within the local community or otherwise. She told herself that she'd really have to start making an effort in that regard, but for the time being, would simply enjoy getting used to their wonderful new home. And it was time to put some effort into reactivating her online business. Now that most of the household goods had been unpacked and put away, she was able to start concentrating on it and she set about organising her studio.

It was when she was sitting at her workbench sorting through her collection of semi-precious stones that, glancing out of the window, Beth noticed a scrawny-looking dog cowering under the yew tree looking, she muttered to herself, longingly, towards the house, and particularly to where Beth was sitting. *Wonder who he belongs to*, she thought. *Poor thing looks half-starved.*

Abandoning what she was doing, Beth wandered outside, crouched down and gently called, 'Here, boy.' The dog needed no further encouragement. It stood and slowly slouched its way towards her. Beth warily reached out her hand and stroked its head. 'Where did you come from then? Are you lost?' It responded by licking her hand. Beth noticed that it didn't have a collar. Her knowledge of dogs, like her knowledge of trees and hedgerows, was limited. The only dog Chris and she had ever owned had been a small rescue dog called Spot when they were children. When it ran into the road and was run over, their parents said they wouldn't risk getting another. But Beth did know enough to guess from this dog's height and longish straggly hair that somewhere in its ancestry was possibly some lurcher or greyhound, or both. She stood up and walked back into the house, intending to bring out a bowl of water before finding the poor thing some scraps. The dog unexpectedly padded along behind her straight into the studio. 'Who said you could come in?' she laughed. The dog stood and looked at her. 'Sit,' Beth ordered, not really expecting it to obey, but to her amazement, the dog obediently sat down, its mournful eyes following her as she made her way over to the little studio kitchen area. On turning back from the sink with a bowl of water and some left-over chicken which she'd intended to have for lunch, she found that the dog had settled himself beside her workbench, looking quite at home. The chicken was gone in a flash, the water was lapped up and then it lay down again as though settling in for a long stay. 'Somebody must be missing you,' Beth said, stroking him gently and letting him once again lick her hand, at the same time wondering if the local vet could help identify the dog's owner. Didn't most dogs have chips these days? Maybe that was why the owner hadn't bothered with a collar.

Beth checked on her laptop for the nearest veterinary surgery, pleased to note that there was one just down the road in the village. She picked up her mobile and explained the situation over the phone. The woman she spoke to suggested that she contact a nearby animal rescue centre who would collect the dog and try to locate the owner. For some reason Beth couldn't explain, other than having found the dog and feeling somehow responsible for him, she wanted to ensure that whoever his owners were, he'd be returning to somewhere he would be loved, and properly looked after. From the state of the dog, she suspected it had been neglected by whomever it belonged to. She eventually managed to persuade the woman to let her bring the dog to the surgery where the vet would be able to check for an identity chip. The arrangement having been made, Beth wondered how she'd get him there without a collar and lead. But, as it turned out, she needn't have worried. As she put on her coat and grabbed her bag and keys, she found that the dog had stood up and followed at her heels. *Maybe no need of a leash*, she thought, and she was right. She simply clicked her fingers, said 'Come on, boy,' and he followed her out of the house and jumped straight into the back seat of the car as though it was the most natural thing in the world.

'Trusting, aren't you?' she said, giving him a pat before getting into the driving seat.

'No chip, I'm afraid,' confirmed the vet. 'So no way to identify him. But, that aside, apart from seeming to be in need of a good feed, he's otherwise in reasonable health for his age, which I'd put at around six or seven years old.'

'So what happens now?' Beth asked.

'Well, the local rescue centre will take him and try to locate the owner.'

'And if the owner can't be found?'

'Then they'll attempt to get him re-housed.'

Beth looked down at the dog waiting patiently at her feet and she could have sworn that he gazed pleadingly back at her as though begging her to take him home with her.

'Look,' said the vet, 'I'm afraid my facilities are all fully occupied with animals requiring treatment at the moment. Do you think you could hold onto him until the rescue centre can send someone out to collect him? Sandra, my receptionist, will give you the number and you can get in touch with them direct.'

Beth instantly agreed, knowing that that wasn't what she intended, and at the same time dismissing any qualms she was having about the abduction of someone else's property. Thanking the vet, she walked back through the reception area, straight past the receptionist and out of the door with the dog obediently following.

Once at the car, she crouched down and hugged the dog, not minding the fact that he was a bit smelly. 'No horrible rescue centre for you,' she whispered. 'Not if I can help it. And anyway, it doesn't look to me like you've been given much affection, or even much sustenance for that matter, by whoever owned you. Though I don't know what Martin will say.' She drove until she spotted a pet shop where, after consultation with the shopkeeper, she bought appropriate dog food and a collar and leash, along with several feeding bowls and a big, cushiony dog bed. Then she drove home. The dog needed no encouragement to follow her inside, settling down, as before, by the workbench.

'Making yourself at home already, I see,' she said as she went about unwrapping her purchases. 'This is where I like to be as well.' She bent down, stroked his shaggy coat, and said, 'A dog after my own heart. We'll need to think of a name, won't we? Can't just call you Dog.' Beth had to admit to herself that it was love at first sight.

***

Beth had just fed the dog and was continuing to unpack her jewellery equipment when Martin arrived home. She'd had high hopes that he'd welcome the presence of a dog, knowing how isolated she was during the day. What she hadn't anticipated was the aggressive low, menacing snarl that greeted Martin as he came in through the internal garage door.

'Jesus, Beth,' he exclaimed, stepping back as the dog got to its feet, hackles raised.

'Shush, Dog,' Beth ordered and was relieved to see that it obediently settled back down on its new bed.

'Where the hell did that come from?' Martin asked, his tone expressing his obvious displeasure.

'Sorry, darling,' Beth said as apologetically as she could, 'I should have thought to warn you. You don't mind, do you? I thought a dog would be a good companion for me while you're out businessing.'

'I wish you'd said, Beth. As far as I recall, I don't remember you ever mentioning that you wanted a dog. If you'd told me then we could have discussed it. Made sure we got a proper dog. Not a scraggy mutt like that bloody thing. A rescue dog, I presume?'

'Yes, of course. You're not really too upset, are you?'

'Of course I'm bloody upset. We could have talked it over it before you took it into your head to just take yourself off to a bloody rescue centre and decide on the ugliest, flea-ridden mutt you could find. And an unfriendly, more than likely fucking dangerous mutt at that!'

'Martin, please don't be angry. I promise you he's as gentle as they come. That's the first growl since I picked him up this morning. I'm sure it's simply because you're unfamiliar to him. He just needs to get to know you.'

'I'm not happy about this, Beth. In fact, to be honest, I'm thoroughly pissed off.' He stormed up the stairs, shouting back as he went, 'I want you to get rid of it.'

'Martin,' Beth called after him, 'please don't walk away. Can't we discuss it like adults rather than petulant children? You're not giving me a chance to explain. And while we're at it, I really don't appreciate you giving me orders. Telling me what I can have and what I can't.'

Martin turned at the top of the stairs, glaring at Beth. She wasn't sure who was most shocked. She couldn't remember ever having stood up for herself the way she did that day. And she wasn't finished. She crossed her arms defensively and shouted up at him. 'The dog's staying, Martin. My mind's made up. You're hardly ever here and therefore have no idea how lonely it can be.' It was then that Martin realised she wasn't going to back down.

'Well, if you're so determined to keep the bloody thing despite my objection,' he said angrily, 'I don't ever want to see it up here. It can bloody well stay down there in your studio. I think you're just being bloody minded, not to mention fucking inconsiderate.'

Martin left Beth in no doubt about the extent of his anger at coming home to find that a dog had appeared seemingly out of the blue, but she was uncharacteristically determined to not back down. She was certain that once he got to know the dog, he'd be fine. She sat on her chair next to the dog, which had settled down again on his cushion, and stroked him gently, wondering at her new-found determination. 'Don't worry,' she said, 'you'll get used to each other. In the meantime, I really will have to think of a name for you.'

As the days went by Martin gradually resigned himself to the presence of the dog in a begrudging sort of way. It being confined to the studio, a room Martin still didn't care to visit, meant that they kept their distance from one another. Beth's hopes that he'd come to love the dog as she did were being slowly crushed, so a sort of truce was agreed, though the atmosphere was strained.

Beth noticed that each time the dog left the house he made straight for the yew. Here he would slump down and rest his head on his paws, for all the world looking forlorn, almost as though pining. After a few days of observing this behaviour and, it being a cold but fine day, Beth grabbed her coat and walked out to join him, sitting herself down beside him under the yew. 'What's wrong, Dog?' she said, gently stroking him behind his ears. He put his head in her lap, a sure sign that he wanted to keep her beside him. 'OK then,' she murmured, 'I could probably do with a bit of a rest.' She still hadn't thought of a suitable name and had begun to simply call him 'Dog'. 'Can't seem to decide on another name for you, Dog,' she said. 'Probably because I'm being too picky.' Dog's ears pricked up and he licked her hand.

As she took her hand away to use the grass to rub off his saliva, her fingers started toying with small bits of gravel and earth, picking up each small pebble and, childlike, amusing herself seeing how far she could throw. She was intrigued when her fingers alighted on a small white chip, very slightly concave on one side. It was smooth to the touch and felt like bone, or a piece of broken china. Beth liked nothing better than making use of found objects and wondered if it would polish up sufficiently to be incorporated into one of her designs. She put it in her pocket, patted Dog on the head and strolled back indoors.

Chapter Twelve

She'll use it, Pickie. She'll make somethin' nice with it and won't be able to let it go. She'll keep and wear part of me. A part that was broken by fists. She's clever, me bonnie. Craftin' and makin' pretty things. Usin' a little piece of me, as though she knows I'm lookin' out for her. Just like she's now lookin' out for me and you. I knew she would. It's taken a long while, Pickie, but it was always goin' to come about, no matter how long the wait. Kin is kin. We know our own. We'll be as one. Her and me. It's sad she'll get to feel some of me pain. But it'll only be for a while. Only until after our work is done. She'll be happy then. After. She'll have a new life. A better life. And there'll be no blame to fall on her. We'll make sure of that. We needed her to bring them all together. Help with the gatherin'. And it's happenin'. It's been set in motion, just as our yew promised. But we need to wait for the others. The one who came after me. The boy brat. The one who was doted on. The one who was wanted. I'll know the one. Be it man or woman, I'll know, won't I, Pickie? How could I not? I couldn't not know the same sly look in those leering eyes as me da's. Me da's eyes what I dreaded seein' and the graspin' hands I didn't have the strength to pull away from in the dead of night when I was just a wee lass. The first user. Da, then Gregory then Sadler. They have to pay, Pickie. Mebbe the yew will release us when we're done, to enjoy what was taken from us. Or mebbe not.

Chapter Thirteen

The planned housewarming was again postponed, due mainly to Martin's sullenness. He'd been that way since Dog had arrived. Beth was keen for the get-together to happen, wanting to spend time getting to know his staff better, particularly Bridget. But her main reason was that she wanted an excuse for Chris to visit. Not that she felt she needed an excuse, but she didn't want to pressure her sister, knowing her workload. Martin remained adamant about postponing, citing work pressures and, on one particular evening, trying to put it down to the fact that there were still a few finishing touches to the house awaiting attention.

'Like what?' Beth quizzed him. She thought she'd made the house as perfect as it could be.

The tone of his response was accusatory. 'There are still several pictures in storage down in the garage which are yet to be hung,' he said, adding, 'You said you'd take care of that, but haven't. And there's still another couple of boxes of books and ornaments yet to go on the shelves.'

Beth went on the defensive. 'Well, you said you'd help with that, but haven't. And, anyway, since when did you become so house-proud and particular?'

'I've been working long hours, in case you haven't noticed, while you've been spending your days giving more attention to that bloody animal than you have to anything else.'

Beth was becoming fearful of the direction their marriage was taking. She'd never known Martin to be churlish in the past, but for the last week or so it seemed to have become the norm. She'd mentioned it over the phone to Chris who hadn't been as supportive as Beth had come to expect.

'I'm sure you're fretting unnecessarily,' Chris had said. 'All married couples have their ups and downs. And, if you think about it, Martin's taken on a lot of responsibility having been entrusted with the setting up of the new agency. He's more than likely just a bit stressed.'

'Honestly, Chris. I think it's more than that. I hardly ever see him, and when I do he's a grumpy sod.'

'Are you sure he's getting enough?' asked Chris.

Beth could detect the lewd grin, even over the phone. 'Trust you to put everything down to sex, or the lack of.'

'Can't deny it, sis.'

'Look, Chris, we're again postponing the housewarming but I'd really like to see you. Any chance you can get away soon?'

'I'll work on it. And listen, I'm sure you're over reacting to what sounds to me like one of those minor marital skirmishes. Lighten up a bit. To be honest, I'm not surprised Martin's a bit pissed off. What were you thinking, just deciding on the spur of the moment to get a dog?'

'Well, it wasn't so much as me getting a dog as a dog getting me.'

'What's that supposed to mean?'

'I lied. He didn't come from a rescue centre. I found him. And it was weird Chris. It was like he was looking for me.'

'What! And you just decided to keep him? Just like that?'

'Yes.'

'I think the move north must have addled your brain. Look, I'll try to get up next weekend. You're beginning to worry me.'

Chapter Fourteen

I was barely fourteen when da heard that the Hill House people were looking for a laundry maid. He sent me there. I don't know why. Tired of me mebbe. Or, more likely, decided it was time I contributed to his coffers. I don't mind tellin' you I was scared. I was so used to me life slaving on the farm. It was the only life I'd known. He sent me on me own. It was a long way to walk with me clumsy foot and by the time I got there I was sweatin'. I'd been rushin' because if I was late and they turned me away I didn't know how I could go back and tell me da. More than likely I'd've been given another batterin', I'd started out with me hair neatly pinned up but by the time I got there it had come loose and I must've looked a right sight. But Mrs Bull took to me. Mebbe took pity on me because of me foot. I liked Mrs Bull. Wished I'd been born to her instead of me excuse for a ma.

Chapter Fifteen

Beth sat at her workbench and pulled the white chip from her pocket, studying it carefully, considering how best to use it. At only a centimetre wide and no more than one and half centimetres long, it was smaller than the pieces she usually worked with. It was definitely going to be a challenge. She carefully filed away the rough edges before carrying on until she'd produced a workable teardrop shape. Once polished to a glossy pearly white, Beth decided it would become the centrepiece of a pendant. Considering it to be too stark to be mounted on its own, she wondered what best to use to give it contrast. Hoping for inspiration, she rummaged through her collection box of semi-precious stones, finally deciding on the small chips of Whitby jet that she'd been wondering what to do with. Beth was already visualising the end result. The white teardrop would be embraced on either side by crescent-shaped shiny jet then mounted and edged with silver to give it more definition. As she sketched out the design, Beth's thoughts kept wandering back to what Chris had said on the phone. Perhaps, on reflection, Chris had been right. Perhaps Beth's own recent attitude had been instrumental in creating the current disharmony. The atmosphere between herself and Martin had been uncomfortably strained and, she reflected, neither she nor Martin had made any effort to arrange to meet for lunch for over a week now. But, then again, wasn't it the case that Chris had often castigated her for being overly meek. For not standing up for herself. Had she taken the advice too far? Beth put her project to one side, suddenly deciding to drive into the city and surprise Martin, hoping it would go some way towards closing the distance that was growing between them.

She walked outside and called for Dog who was in his usual place beneath the yew. Once inside, he went straight to his basket by the bench and settled, instinctively seeming to know that Beth was going out.

Since that first day, Dog had only ever left Beth's side to go and lie under the yew or to wander around the grounds, never seeming to want to stray further. She marvelled at her good fortune in finding such a devoted and obedient companion. It was just a pity that Martin didn't feel the same way.

***

Bridget was alone in the office and her face lit up when she saw Beth. 'Hello, stranger,' she beamed at Beth. 'Come to tempt him to lunch, I hope,' she said.

'Was hoping to, Bridget, unless he's busy.'

Bridget closed the file she'd been working on and hesitated slightly before leaning conspiratorially closer to Beth, a concerned look on her face. 'I'm pleased you've come in, Beth. I don't mean to be a busybody or to interfere in any way, but to be honest Martin hasn't been his usual cheery self these last couple of weeks,' she whispered, even though they were alone. 'I hope nothing's wrong.'

'Actually, Bridget, I have to admit that I think that's my fault. I got myself a dog a few weeks ago without telling him and they don't seem to like each other. But I am a bit worried about him. As you say, he's not been his usual chirpy self. I thought maybe pressure of work was getting to him. How's it going, anyway? Business, I mean. Martin hasn't been giving me the usual updates lately.'

'Well, as far as sales go, it couldn't be better. I've worked for a few estate agents over the years and have to admit that your husband certainly knows his stuff. We're already over this month's target and we still have another week to go. That's why it's so odd that he seems to have a case of the doldrums. Hopefully seeing you will cheer him up a bit.'

'That's what I'm hoping too. Where is he, anyway?'

'He should be back any time now. He's been out on a viewing but he called in just before you arrived to say he was on his way back.'

Beth sat down on one of the plush chairs in the reception area and for the first time really noticed the attractive layout and decor. It had the air of calm efficiency and professionalism. Quite an achievement. She knew that Martin had been given free rein to arrange and furnish the place and she wondered how, given his self-acknowledged lack of talent in that department, he'd achieved such a successful result. She mentioned it to Bridget.

There was a hint of something akin to disdain in her voice when Bridget said, 'I believe — no, in fact I *know* — that Martin entrusted most of it to the multi-talented Fiona.' Sniffing in disapproval, she added, 'It seems that woman applies the same dedication to interior design as she does to her own appearance. I don't mean to be unkind but I'm afraid I find her too pushy by half.'

'Bridget!' Beth exclaimed, but there was a hint of smile on her face. 'I gather you've not taken to the multi-talented Fiona.'

Bridget had the grace to look a trifle shame-faced at her indiscretion, but it didn't stop her adding, 'Speak as you find,' at which point Martin entered, closely followed by Fiona.

Beth got the uncomfortable impression that neither were too pleased to see her. She hoped it was her imagination going haywire.

***

Beth linked her arm through Martin's as they strolled down to the Market Tavern in the square, grateful that he didn't pull away. Bracing herself, she said, 'I'm sorry, Martin, I know it was unacceptable for me to get Dog without any consultation. Forgive me? Please?'

'It's like you've become someone else, Beth. Did you think that because I was happy for you to not only insist on the location of the house, despite my initial doubts, deny me any input on the design, me having no sense of style, he made quote marks in the air, that I'd be happy with your own personal choice of dog without any attempt at consultation. A dog which, incidentally, I remain unhappy with.' He stressed the word *unhappy*. 'I've noticed a change in you these last months, Beth. We always used to at least make a show of making life-changing decisions together. I never thought selfishness was in your psyche. I've always loved you for your consideration. Your willingness to compromise. You're gradually succeeding in making me feel redundant. Pretty worthless, in fact.'

'Jesus,' Martin,' Beth said. 'I don't know what to say. Other than sorry. I honestly didn't realise my behaviour was that upsetting. Have I really been that selfish? No, don't answer that. You have every right to be upset. In my defence, I can only say that my thoughtlessness was unintentional. I suppose I just didn't think. What, with you being so busy with the setting up and running of the new office, I just took it upon myself to make decisions without you. I realise now that it was unforgivable.'

'So you'll get rid of the dog?'

'I can't do that, Martin. Please don't ask me to. It would be too cruel.'

'Right then.' Martin glared at Beth and marched into the pub ahead of her. Lunch was a quiet affair.

***

Arriving home, Dog, as usual, was waiting behind the door to greet her. She fed and petted him then set to work on the pendant, sad that her apology hadn't improved things between her and Martin. But, she thought, it was unreasonable for him to insist on getting rid of Dog. 'It's not going to happen,' she muttered, leaning down and stroking his rough hair.

Only partially successful in managing to put aside the disappointment she felt in being unable to reinstate marital harmony, Beth sat down at her work table and set about shaping the little pieces of jet that would form part of the pendant.

Chapter Sixteen

When the young master Gregory arrived home from his travels he waited little time before singlin' me out. I was barely fifteen but I could tell what he was after. I'd seen the same look in the greedy eyes of me da. I did me best to avoid Gregory as much as I could but he got his way in the end, creeping into me poky little attic room in the middle of the night. Who could I tell? He knew I'd be called a liar. He would deny it and who would be believed? I'd be sent packin'. I'd have no choice other than to go back to the farm and me bastard da. That would have been worse than putting up with Gregory's fumblin'. At least he pretended to have some affection for me and didn't call me a cripple, at least not to me face. And I was never afeared of getting a beltin' from him. But then he was just as bad in his way when all's said and done, the way he treated me in the end. And the mistress. She was no better. I hope he suffered throughout the rest of his days, though I doubt it. He more than likely continued to live out his life in the comfort afforded by wealth and privilege, more's the pity.

Chapter Seventeen

Beth was excited, as well as relieved, on Saturday morning, getting ready to pick up Chris from the station. Standing in the doorway, she picked up her keys and called for Dog to come inside. As usual, he came as soon as she called but instead of moving past her to make way to his basket, he circled her legs just as she was about to step outside. Not expecting it, Beth stumbled, only managing to remain upright by grasping the edge of the big oak door, but not managing to avoid a painful knock to her cheek bone. She put her fingers against her cheek and found that she was bleeding slightly. *So blinking clumsy of me*, she thought and moved back into the studio bathroom to check the damage. Looking at herself in the mirror she was relieved to discover it was only a small graze. Nevertheless, she knew there'd be a bit of a bruise. She reached the station just as Chris's train was pulling in.

'Jesus, Beth!' Chris exclaimed. 'What have you done now?'

'What?'

Chris pointed to Beth's cheekbone. 'Last time it was a bruise on your arm, and now you turn up with an injury to your face.'

'Oh, that,' answered Beth. 'Just a little accident this morning. Clumsy of me, really. Dog got in the way and I stumbled. It's nothing.'

'OK, if you say so, but it doesn't look like nothing to me. It's turning into a bit of a shiner.'

'Honestly, it's fine, Chris. Now, what do you want to do? Martin insists on working Saturdays and won't be home until around five so we've got several hours to kill.'

'Well, much as I want to see the finished house and meet this dog of yours, I'm dying for some decent coffee. The stuff on the train is bloody undrinkable.'

Beth parked the car in Prince Bishops car park and they wandered down to Café Nero.

'So, little big sister,' said Chris once they were settled. 'What's been going on since we last had a little heart-to-heart? Is all well on the marriage front?'

'It could be worse I suppose, Chris.' Beth paused. 'Getting Dog probably wasn't the best move I ever made. Martin definitely resents my choice. I don't think he was against having a dog. He just doesn't like this particular dog. And Dog hasn't taken to Martin either, which is not surprising given that Martin ignores him completely.'

'And I don't suppose you'd get rid of the dog for the sake of marital harmony.'

'Absolutely not. I couldn't do that to Dog. He dotes on me. It would be a terrible betrayal of his trust. And anyway, I love him.'

'More than Martin?'

'Don't be daft, Chris. You know Martin means the world to me.'

'Well, I'm sure they'll both come round in time. Martin's not one to bear a grudge. Is he still working mega long hours?'

'I'm afraid so. Though I don't know why he can't let up a bit. According to Bridget, business is booming, to the extent they're considering taking on a junior administrator and maybe another negotiator. Come to think of it, perhaps that's what's needed for him to be able to ease off a bit. Extra staff.'

'There you go then! The poor man's overworked. He needs to have some fun to bring him out of himself. And there's no better time than the weekend, so tonight's on me. And I won't take no for an answer. Just picked up a bit of a bonus so I'm feeling flush. I think the two of you need cheering up so I suggest you get your thinking cap on and let's plan a bloody good night out.'

'God, I love you, Chris. You always know how to raise my spirits. Though I have to say that I'm not sure about a full-blown night on the town. Not your sort of night on the town anyway. I don't have your staying power. Would you settle for dinner and drinks in a decent local restaurant?'

'Fine, if that's what you want. And you know me. As long as the wine's flowing, I'm happy anywhere.'

They finished their coffee and strolled back to the car park.

When they arrived home, Dog gave his usual enthusiastic welcome to Beth before having a good sniff at Chris, obviously deciding she was of little consequence.

'God, it's incredible,' Chris commented as they entered the living room, 'but I might find myself agreeing with Martin when it comes to the dog. He's not the most attractive of creatures.'

'True. But, as you well know, beauty is in the eye of the beholder, and, to me, he's beautiful.'

'There's no accounting for taste, I suppose,' Chris quipped.

'Sadly, he still seems to regard Martin as the enemy. And he'd be right, of course. Martin would get rid of him in a flash given half the chance. Come on, let me show you your bedroom.'

Admiration expressed, Beth grabbed a bottle of chardonnay and they settled on the lounge sofas.

The talk mainly centred on Chris's London life, her PR job and her latest sexual conquests. Beth wondered if Chris would ever settle down and, if she eventually did, would she become bored once the novelty of cohabiting wore off. It was beginning to look that way as far as Beth's own life was concerned. Was it her? Or was it Martin? Or was it a combination of both?'

'What's up sis?' asked Chris, noticing the contemplative look on her sister's face during a lull in the conversation.

'I'm not sure,' answered Beth. 'I suppose now that I seem to have reached a point where I have everything I ever dreamed of, the reality somehow isn't living up to that dream. I know that must sound incredibly ungrateful. Just don't know what's wrong with me, Chris. I feel permanently discontented these days.'

Chris moved over and sat down beside her sister. 'Listen, Beth,' she said, 'over the last God knows how many months, both you and Martin have been living different but equally busy and stressful lives. Martin's doing his utmost to ensure his future and you've been occupied with creating this beautiful home. Now that everything's going so well, maybe it's time you both took a break. Have a proper holiday.'

Beth looked doubtful.

'Or if that's not possible at the moment, at least organise a long weekend. Buy yourself some sexy underwear. Gee things up a bit. Believe me, I've always seen you two as the perfectly matched, happy-ever-after couple, and I can't believe this little blip can't be sorted. There's nothing else bothering you is there?'

Beth didn't reply.

'Come on! Spill! What is it?'

Just then they heard Dog growling and barking, followed by the sound of the rollers going up on the garage door.

The moment for confidences was lost as they waited for Martin's entrance through the internal garage door. As he walked over to give Chris his usual hug of greeting, he scowled at Beth saying, 'I hope you've noticed how much that bloody animal hates me. Hi, Chris. I take it you've met the savage addition to our dream home. Did it give you the same welcome it bloody well gives me every time I come home?'

'Hi, Martin. Lovely to see you too.'

'Sorry, Chris. Long week. Anyway, it's great to see you too.'

He flopped onto the sofa next to Chris. 'Anything on the agenda for tonight?'

'Getting stuffed and getting pissed, the usual shenanigans when I'm around,' answered Chris.

'Thank Christ for that! I'm in need of a bloody good piss-up. Where do you reckon? Better order a taxi if we're going into Durham.'

Beth moved across to give him a peck on the cheek. 'No need,' she said. 'Already booked a table at the local Italian if that's OK by you. The walk will help us build up an appetite.'

'Fine by me.' Martin stood up and took himself off to shower and change.

Chris raised her eyebrows at Beth. 'Hm, not the happy chappie I'm used to.'

'Tell me about it,' answered Beth.

Twenty minutes later, Dog safely shut in the studio, they made their way down the hill to the village, Martin striding ahead, making for The Kings Head to get a few in before dinner.

While Martin was at the bar ordering their drinks, Chris's eyes alighted on the pendant Beth was wearing. 'Your latest creation?'

'Yes. The only thing I've made so far since moving in. I've decided to keep it. What do you think?'

'Suits you,' answered Chris, 'although I'm not too sure about the stark mix of black and white. I'm all for a bit of colour, myself. It's unusual though.' Chris frowned then asked, 'Have you thought about the symbolism of the two colours together?'

'Not really, but I'm sure you're about to enlighten me.'

'Black and white. Good and evil. Purity and depravity. Life and death, etcetera.'

'Enough, Chris! I wish I hadn't asked. You're freaking me out. It never occurred to me to explore any mythical or otherwise connection between the colours. I just like the contrast. Anyway, together they make grey, which is a positive way of looking at things. Neither good nor bad. Seeing both sides. Not being judgmental.'

Martin returned with their drinks and proceeded to knock back his pint. 'What's this about not being judgmental?' he asked.

'Oh, we were just discussing Beth's most recent creation. The pendant,' said Chris, pointing to it. 'What do you think, Martin?'

'Haven't really got an opinion, lacking taste as I do,' Martin answered, looking pointedly at Beth.

Chris sensed the slightly confrontational atmosphere and rapidly changed the subject.

'What about this house-warming then? Made a date yet?' she asked. 'I'm looking forward to a party, as always.'

'I've been too busy to give it much thought,' Martin replied, then got up to get them all a refill.'

The conversation faltered after that, despite Chris's attempts to lighten the mood. She downed her drink and said, 'About time to eat, I think, before the booze starts to take hold and I become an embarrassment, a state you've both been witness to oft times in the past.' She looked across at her sister thinking it a bit strange that Martin hadn't commented on the injury to Beth's face. An unpleasant thought briefly entered her head but she rapidly dismissed it. Knowing Martin as she did, it was simply unthinkable. They drank up and made their way to the restaurant.

Chapter Eighteen

The woman's not one of them, Pickie. She's no threat. Even though she's a bit too full of herself, as me ma would say. I wasn't allowed to be too full of meself. Good for nothin' is what she always told me I was. But I was good for somethin', wasn't I, Da, you filthy old bugger. And good for Gregory as well until I wasn't. Then good for the Sadler bastard that you gave me to. Aye, you gave me to him even though I didn't want to go. No. You didn't give me to him. You'd not give somethin' for nowt'. Even somethin' you didn't want. You sold me. The blame for what happened wasn't mine. It was yours, yours, yours. It all started with you. Did you know how much I hated you, Da? And still do. I told you once. Do you remember? Only the once it was, and I didn't mind the beatin'. It was worth it.

Chapter Nineteen

The restaurant was full with diners making the most of their Saturday night. Beth was congratulating herself on having had the good sense to book in advance, and Chris was relieved to note that during the short walk from the pub the atmosphere she'd sensed earlier between Martin and Beth seemed to have slightly improved. With all three busy studying the menus, they hadn't noticed the table of four women near the back until one left her seat and headed in their direction. A perfectly manicured hand was suddenly clamped onto Martin's shoulder.

'Martin, what a lovely surprise,' simpered Fiona, looking seductively stylish as she bent to give Martin a peck on the cheek.

Both Beth and Chris noticed that Martin was blushing as he stood to greet her, but there was no doubting the surprise on his face. 'What are you doing in this neck of the woods, then?' he asked. 'I thought you lived on the other side of Durham.'

'Well, I do, but I'm here enjoying an evening out with some girlfriends, one of whom is local to the area.'

Martin recovered himself sufficiently to remember his manners. 'You know Beth of course,' he said, 'and this is my sister-in-law, Chris. Chris, this is my colleague, Fiona.'

Chris was about to say something along the lines that it was nice to meet someone who worked alongside Martin but Fiona simply nodded briefly in their direction, appearing to dismiss them out of hand, before turning back to Martin and saying, 'Look Martin, this is an opportunity not to be missed. I happen to be staying in the village tonight with my friend so I'm not going to be in any rush after dinner. Why don't we all meet up afterwards for a drink? Make a bit of a party of it?'

Martin turned to Beth and Chris for help, looking pointedly from one to the other with a barely discernible shake of the head and silently mouthing 'Help.'

'I'm afraid that won't be possible Fiona,' said Beth. 'We have an early start tomorrow morning so sadly we'll have to pass.'

Fiona pouted in disappointment. 'Does that include you as well, Martin?' she said. 'Do you have to have an early start as well?'

'Unfortunately, that's right,' Martin said. 'Chris has an early train to catch, and then Beth and I have already made plans for the day, so it's a no-go I'm afraid, Fiona. Sorry.'

Fiona frowned, making a show of her disappointment. 'We'll have to make it some other time then. Anyway, see you on Monday.' She gave a sexy little wave and made her way back to her friends, who had been eyeing Martin with undisguised interest.

'Who the hell is that?' whispered Chris, once Fiona was safely out of hearing range.

'As I said, a colleague,' Martin whispered back.

'Can't say I warmed to her,' said Chris with a look of distaste.

Martin nodded his agreement 'Not many do,' he said, 'but I'm afraid she's bloody good at her job so I have to keep her on-side.'

'Well done on fending her off, but you do know, don't you, that I'm here until Monday,' said Chris.

'Yes, but she doesn't know that,' he answered, grinning.

They both noted that Beth had gone quiet.

'Are you all right, darling?' asked Martin. 'You look a bit pale.'

'I'm fine. Just concentrating on the menu. What have you decided to have Chris?'

But Beth wasn't fine. She was chilled. She'd seen the look Fiona had given Martin. It was predatory. And she had a vague memory of having seen that look before. A long time ago. Sometime before the move north. But that was impossible. She'd only met Fiona recently. The feeling stayed with her throughout the evening, even when Martin and Chris, fuelled by alcohol, sang their usual medley of old Stones' hits, all the way home.

Chapter Twenty

See, Pickie. We're almost there. The coming together will soon be complete. I couldn't not know that look. The look that says 'I'll have what I want, whatever the cost'. The look that's been handed down through the generations. Gregory. Underneath, this one's just the same. For seven long months Gregory would creep up to me room to make use of me. He whispered small kindnesses as he raised me shift and entered me. Why should he have bothered with kindnesses? It would've made no difference. Da never bothered with kindnesses. So you see, Pickie, I believed Master Gregory had some affection for me. I was young. I wanted it to be so. After a while I even began to think I loved him. Fool that I was. I remember that horrible day when I happened upon him and the mistress talkin' on the landing. Her telling him that she'd been made aware of his nightly visits to the room of the cripple. That's what she called me, Pickie. Just the same as da. Mind you, I heard no malice in the word when said by the mistress. Da always said it in a way that made me feel worthless. I couldn't move then. I needed to hear what Gregory would say. So I heard the whole conversation. I heard the amusement in Gregory's voice when he said, 'A little trivial dalliance, Mama. Nothing more than that, and nothing to worry about.'

'But I do worry, Gregory. And it must stop,' she ordered.

'How else is a man to gain experience, Mama?' he said.

I remember peekin' round the corner then and seein' the smirk on his face.

'Can a man go to his bride without knowledge of the intimacies expected of him?'

'Knowledge to be gained somewhere other than his own household, Gregory,' the mistress replied. Her voice was stern and I couldn't imagine anybody darin' to go against her wishes. If she'd spoke to me like that I would've been quakin' in me boots. 'You must curb your urges,' she ordered. 'Your uncle arrives next week. You will raise the matter with him and he will advise. Your papa will wish to remain ignorant of the issue and I will not raise the matter with him. I fully understand the needs of a young man, but I value the girl's expertise and industry. I don't want to lose her. But if you continue, I shall have no choice.' Turnin' her back on him she said, 'Now, we'll consider the matter closed.'

When they'd gone, I stood for a minute or two, hands covering' me distended belly. I'd said nothing to Gregory about me lack of bleedin's. Me fillin' out. I can't begin to describe me fear, Pickie. Ma's lyin' in time had almost come. I knew what the swellin' was. I'd watched the ruttin' of the ram on the ewes. Watched the *lambin' as well. I fretted summat awful about what would happen to me. I said nothin' to Gregory, but he knew all right. He knew and he didn't care. He kept comin'.*

Chapter Twenty-One

On Sunday morning, Martin and Chris agreed to Beth's suggestion to take a drive over to the north east coast, choosing Tynemouth as their destination. After a pleasant drive, they were delighted to come across the indoor market which they subsequently learnt was a regular event held each Sunday in the pretty railway station. The place was bustling with activity and they couldn't help but be impressed by the wide array of goods on offer, as well as the variety of street food to be had. Beth's eye was caught by a stall selling beautiful, colourful silk scarves. There were so many different designs to choose from. She turned to Chris, saying, 'If you were to choose one, Chris, which one would you go for?' After a few minutes of consideration, Chris, as Beth had expected, picked out the most brightly coloured one she could find. Duly wrapped and paid for, Beth handed it to Chris. 'Present,' she said, smiling.

'Really? What have I done to deserve this? asked Chris as Beth handed it over.

'Just for being you.' Beth hugged her sister. 'I don't know what I'd do without you.'

'Well, that's never going to happen, is it, you silly bugger. You know I'll always be there for you.'

'Hence the silk scarf, so say, *thank you, Beth, it's very kind of you.*'

'Thank you, Beth, it's very kind of you.'

They wandered on, arm in arm, Martin trailing behind, being more interested in old war memorabilia than silk scarves or antique jewellery, which was what Beth and Chris were now looking at.

The stallholder, an elderly, wizened woman, herself bedecked with what appeared to be expensive gold necklaces and fistfuls of flashy rings, was eyeing Beth's jet and bone necklace.

'That's an interesting little piece you have there, love,' she said. 'I recognise the jet, but what's the white?'

Beth fingered the pendant. 'I'm not sure,' she replied. 'Something I found. I make jewellery, so I thought I'd use it to make this. Do you like it?'

'More's to the point, do you like it, lovie?'

'Oh dear, I'm guessing it's not to your taste.'

The old woman looked straight at Beth and said, 'You'll be all right love.'

'What's that supposed to mean?' piped up Chris, frowning at the woman.

'I just see what I see.' The woman turned back to Beth and said, 'But as I said, you're going to be all right, love. Someone's looking out for you.'

At that, the woman turned away to deal with a customer who was beckoning her over.

'Mad old bitch,' commented Chris as they moved on. 'I'll bet she spouts similar nonsense to anyone who'll listen. Probably thinks she's got some sort of 'gift' or something.'

'Hm,' said Beth, 'the gift of disquieting people. Come on, let's find Martin and grab something to eat.'

But Beth realised she *was* disquieted. The words of the old woman had sounded somehow sinister or prophetic. She wondered about the odd feelings she'd been experiencing over the past months. The fact that she'd been inexplicably drawn to the spot where she immediately knew she wanted her studio to be. Her uncontrollable rage at Martin, when he'd balked at entering the designated space, the feeling of disquiet on meeting Harold, her uncharacteristic rash behaviour in adopting Dog without consultation, and her antagonistic feelings towards Fiona, who she couldn't help feeling she'd come across sometime in her past, or who at least reminded her of something unpleasant. And, now, the disturbing words of the old stallholder. Thinking about it, it all seemed really weird. But it also seemed ridiculous, so she put her thoughts aside and said nothing to either Chris or Martin.

***

After the previous evening's over-indulgence, and the effects of the sea air, all agreed on a light supper of cheese and dips and whatever else could be rustled up from the contents of the fridge, before deciding to call it a night. Martin took himself off to bed while Beth, accompanied by Chris, went downstairs to let Dog out for a few minutes before locking him in for the night. As they stood waiting for Dog to reappear, Chris asked, 'Have you ever thought about the history of this place? I don't just mean the history of Lanchester itself, but of this particular piece of land that you've settled on. Who were the previous owners? Do you know?'

'All I know is what Martin's told me, which is that it was unoccupied for decades before we came along. Apparently, the last owner was a farmer called Sadler and when he died, I think sometime in the nineteen thirties, the property should have passed to his two sons. But it seems all attempts over the years to locate either of them came to nothing. Rumour has it that each son deserted the homestead as soon as he was able, and was never heard from again. So here we are. We have a property that's been untended for almost a hundred years. That's as much as I've been able to find out. Fascinating when you think about it. But actually, you've now raised my curiosity about the history of the rest of Lanchester.'

'Planning to do some research?

'Do you know, Chris, I think I will. Especially as I seem to have a lot of time on my hands at the moment. It's not as though commissions have been flooding in since we moved. Not that I've spent a great deal of time on marketing. That's something I should get to grips with soon.'

Dog obediently returned when called and they climbed the stairs to the first floor, having first shut him in the studio.

Chris turned as they were halfway up. 'And by the way, Beth, I don't want to put ideas in your head, but if I were you, I'd keep an eye on that woman.'

'Which woman?' Beth was momentarily confused.

'Fiona, or whatever her name is. She's far too familiar with Martin for my liking.'

'You're not suggesting that Martin would cheat on me, are you Chris?'

'Of course not. But I know how unworldly and trusting you are. I just thought I'd make you aware that she's got her eye on him, and you shouldn't underestimate women like her, which I know to my cost!'

***

Having never before had any doubts about Martin's fidelity, Beth dismissed Chris's warning about Fiona out of hand. She just couldn't believe that Martin would ever cheat on her. But her curiosity about the history of the village had definitely been aroused. She determined to find out more, and decided she would concentrate on the last hundred years or so rather than the ancient history, which, in any case, was well documented and readily available. She would start by exploring the grand properties on the outskirts of the village, especially having been intrigued by one particular big old mansion house which stood alone at the top of a hill leading up to the A68, the old Roman road which stretches from Darlington to Edinburgh. She had passed the house several times when taking trips of discovery to places of interest, one of her favourite destinations being Corbridge, another ancient settlement and a magnet for tourists.

On Monday morning, having dropped Chris at the station, Beth pulled up outside the old wrought iron gates, now chained and rusted. A dull brass plaque, mounted on one of the stone pillars and pitted with age, was engraved with the name, Hill House. Beyond, what must at one time have been the main carriageway, was now almost totally overgrown with weeds, moss and shrubbery until, about ten metres in, she could see a tall, sturdy wooden fence, and beyond that the upper windows of the house itself. Standing there, Beth suddenly experienced a fleeting sense of déjà vu, the same as she'd first experienced in the corner of the studio where she now worked. A sense that she'd been here before. The feeling lingered for moments longer than she was comfortable with. She forced herself to shrug it off, knowing it for the impossibility it undoubtedly was. Getting back in the car, Beth determined to do some research, feeling pretty certain that such a distinguished house would be documented in the old parish records.

Chapter Twenty-Two

Did you see that, Pickie? She felt it. Even though she doesn't know it. She felt the connection. Right back to where she was made. All the way through the generations back to me. I didn't want me first and only wee bairn to come back. I wouldn't have wanted her to know how she came about. And I didn't want her back. I didn't want her to have the life I'd had. But this one. This child is special. The yew is clever, greedy as she is for nourishment. She brought me babbie to us. And me babbie will draw the others. The yew was relieved to have us put here. She'd gone too long without purpose. Made him make his big mistake by bringing us to her. He was beckoned that night by the yearning of the yew.

Chapter Twenty-Three

Fiona wanted Martin. It was a simple fact. The attraction had been there from the start as far as she was concerned. She just needed to make Martin realise it. The fact that he was married was of no consequence. How could that little ineffective woman think she could hold on to him now that Fiona was on the scene? Whether the fascination was destined to be temporary or not didn't bother Fiona. Whenever she'd got bored in the past, she'd always simply moved on. In the meantime, she would use whatever means available to her to achieve her goal. So far, Martin hadn't succumbed, or indeed hadn't even seemed to notice Fiona's advances, or was trying hard to ignore them, so she decided it was time to move things along a notch. A visit to the wife might be in order.

***

Now that the house was finished, Beth thought it was time to do something with the land, but having spent so much on the house there was no possibility for the moment of considering professional landscaping. And with winter approaching, it would more than likely be useless to attempt any sort of proper work until the spring. She decided that, for the time being, it would be enough to simply plant some spring bulbs in pots placed just outside the door. They'd be cheery to look at once the worst of the winter was over. It was as she was just starting to plant the last half dozen bulbs that a car pulled up the drive. She was surprised, and not a little put out, to see that it was Fiona. Beth was dressed in an old pair of jeans and wearing one of Martin's cast-off jumpers several sizes too big. Not the sort of impression she wanted to present to the immaculate Fiona. She pushed the thought aside. Why on earth was she concerned about what Fiona thought? And then it hit her. The only reason she could think of that would warrant a visit from one of Martin's colleagues was that something must have happened to Martin. Why else would Fiona be here? She stood up, trowel in hand, as Fiona got out of the car, attired and coiffed as usual.

'What's happened?' asked Beth, attempting to subdue her rising panic as Fiona approached.

'What do you mean, what's happened? I was simply passing and, as I'm a good half hour early for my next appointment, I thought I'd drop by in the hope of a free cup of coffee. Thought you might welcome a bit of company. Is that, OK? Anyway, I've been curious about this marvellous house that Martin's been raving about.'

Despite her reluctance to entertain Fiona, and finding her fears unwarranted, Beth didn't want to seem rude so felt she had no choice other than to oblige.

'Of course, Fiona. This is such an unexpected pleasure. Come inside and I'll get the kettle on.'

As Beth turned to lead Fiona into the house, Dog appeared as if from nowhere, teeth bared and emitting a low and menacing snarl. Fiona stood stock still, her face white with shock.

'Dog!' Beth ordered firmly, clicking her fingers and pointing to the doorway, the sign for Dog to go inside. He slouched past the frozen Fiona, the snarl reduced to a barely audible guttural growl. Beth locked him in the studio and returned to apologise for his odd behaviour.

'I'm so sorry, Fiona. I don't know what got into him. He's not usually like that, not even with the postman or delivery people, or anyone else for that matter. I can only apologise. Are you all right?'

Fiona was shaking. 'It can't get out again, can it?' she asked shakily.

'No, no. I promise you. He's safely locked away. Come in and I'll get you that coffee. You look like you could do with it.'

Fiona followed Beth inside, her eyes darting about, taking in every detail as they moved through the hall and on up the stairs. Beth was expecting at least a complimentary comment or two. Or even a criticism. But Fiona said nothing. Once in the lounge she settled herself on the sofa. Fiona's silence as she surveyed her surroundings was making Beth uncomfortable so she moved quickly into the kitchen to prepare the coffee, at a loss as to how to make small talk. When she came back, she set the tray down on the coffee table. Fiona still hadn't said anything and Beth assumed she must be in shock after her encounter with Dog. She felt the need to cut the uncomfortable silence, even though she resented Fiona taking it upon herself to pop in out of the blue. And, from the look on Fiona's face, she wasn't looking all that happy to be here either. Beth was curious to know the real reason for the visit, not for one minute believing that Fiona had just been passing.

'Things going well at work, Fiona?' Beth eventually asked, needing to say something.

'Wonderful,' came the reply. 'Couldn't be better, in fact. Martin and I get along like a house on fire.'

'As I'm sure he does with the rest of the team,' Beth said. 'Martin always speaks very highly of you all.' Beth was recalling Chris's comment about Fiona, and starting to believe she might have been right.

Fiona took a sip of her coffee, settled back on the sofa and crossed her long, shapely legs. She looked directly at Beth and said, 'Well, it wouldn't be right to show favouritism, of course. Martin's much too professional for that. But he certainly appreciates the fact that I produce quality business, and he admitted that he couldn't have done without my input during the setting up of the office. Neither Harold nor Malcolm could have achieved that.' She paused, then added, 'And as for Bridget!'

'What about Bridget?' Beth asked, knowing from Fiona's tone that she was about to hear something detrimental.

'Well, you've seen her. Such a frump. No style at all. She wouldn't have been my choice for a front of house role.'

Resenting Fiona's petty criticism of Bridget, Beth countered with, 'I'm not sure style counts for that much, Fiona. What I've noticed is that Bridget's a friendly, welcoming presence to potential clients and certainly appears to be extremely efficient at her job.'

'Anyway,' Fiona went on, 'when Martin took me out to lunch last week, he commented on how indispensable I was to the success of the branch, even going so far as to indicate that should a second north-east branch be considered, he would certainly recommend me above anyone else for the job.'

'I'm sure he values you highly, Fiona, and Martin will always give credit where credit's due.' Beth was becoming frustrated with the self-aggrandizing and wished Fiona would take her leave. Hoping to speed things along, Beth glanced at the time and said, 'Won't you be late for your meeting? You've already been here for almost half an hour. I don't want to keep you.'

To Beth's relief, Fiona stood, straightened her figure-hugging skirt and picked up her oversized bag.

'Yes, I suppose you're right. Well, thanks for the coffee, and no doubt we'll see each other again soon.'

Beth followed Fiona down the stairs, aware of the repeat of that guttural low growl coming from behind the closed studio door as Fiona made her way out.

On the doorstep, Fiona turned, a scowl on her face, and said, 'That animal's savage, Beth. I think you should consider swapping it for something less dangerous, like a rottweiler!'

Beth stood on the doorstep as Fiona drove back down the drive, thinking, *What the hell was that all about?* She released Dog from the studio. After licking Beth's hand and getting a reciprocal fondle behind the ears, Dog wandered back to his spot under the yew while Beth finished planting the rest of the bulbs. She thought about the number of people who had been to the house since they'd moved in. Apart from the usual deliveries and the postman, and of course Chris, she could recall only one other. She and James had worked so well together during the construction that they'd carried on their friendship after the house was finished. He would occasionally pop in to see how the interior space was working out and to admire their joint handiwork. And often simply to indulge in pleasant general chit chat. Beth was always glad to see him, and always a bit sad to see him go. Being alone most of the day, she relished the easy camaraderie of his visits. Thinking about Dog's behaviour, Beth couldn't recall Dog acting with James or anyone else the way he had with Fiona. And apart from those first few days, he and Martin seemed to have arrived at some sort of grudging suspension of hostilities. Admittedly, there was no love lost between them, but they'd come to tolerate one another. Dog's aggressive behaviour towards Fiona was strange, to say the least. But Beth couldn't help but smile to herself as she decided that Dog was obviously an excellent judge of character.

Later, standing in the kitchen chopping vegetables in preparation for the evening meal, Beth's thoughts kept drifting back to Fiona. If, as Chris had suggested, Fiona had her sights set on Martin, could she really be considered a threat? Beth had never considered herself to be of the jealous sort. Admittedly, up until now, she'd never believed she had cause to be. But Fiona was attractive in a sophisticated, man-eating kind of way. And Martin had lately been distracted and not as loving as she would have liked, the onset of his apparent discontent seeming to coincide with the time she found Dog. Well, if there was one thing of which she was certain, it was that Dog was here to stay. Anyway, surely Dog couldn't be the only reason. Turning her thoughts back to Fiona, and especially Chris's assessment of her, Beth was growing increasingly uneasy. The woman certainly had glamour, a quality Beth had long since given up attempting to achieve, considering it unattainable. But had she let herself go that much? It was true that lately she hadn't bothered much to dress up or apply make-up, except when she was taking a trip out. She dropped what she was doing and went into the bedroom to take a long, hard look at herself in the full-length mirror, deciding there and then to make more of an effort. She went back and finished what she needed to do in the kitchen, showered, washed and dried her hair, then carefully applied a little make-up. Finally, after rifling through her wardrobe, she opted for the dark green knee-length dress that Martin had always liked. The black and white pendant complemented the outfit perfectly.

When Martin arrived home a couple of hours later than expected and looking worn out, Beth tried not to show her disappointment when he failed to notice her efforts.

'A tiring day, darling?' she asked sympathetically as she kissed him hello.

Martin sighed. 'Not one of the best, to be honest. Staff bickering is something I hoped never to have to deal with. Bloody women!' he exclaimed before plumping himself down on the sofa and removing his tie.

'Do you want to talk about it?' asked Beth.

'Not really, although suffice to say that Bridget and Fiona tend to not see eye-to-eye. Each seems to be determined to blame the other for anything that doesn't go according to plan.' He let out a weary sigh. 'At least while they're at each other's throats, I suppose it gives young Malcolm a bit of respite. Up until now, he was the one in the firing line when things went awry. You know, Beth, until I got to run my own branch, I hadn't really considered the difficulties of managing trivial in-house bitching. I find myself getting frustrated with the bloody pettiness of it all.'

'Who's accusing who?'

'For the last week or so Fiona's criticisms have focused on Bridget, which in some ways is an improvement on her focusing on Malcolm. Bridget's tough, she bites back. And therein lies the problem.'

'Speaking of Fiona, did you know she dropped by here today?'

'What! Why would she do that? I hadn't rated you two as best buddies. Anyway, what did she want?' Martin was genuinely surprised. He was also a bit worried. So far, he'd managed to stave off Fiona's advances, but she was an attractive woman and it was becoming increasingly difficult. He had to admit he was tempted. Now what was she up to? He'd never anticipated that there might come a time when he'd find himself again hankering after anyone other than Beth but, lately, he'd begun to wonder.

'I think she was just being nosy. She didn't mention it then?'

'No. Didn't say a word. So what reason did she give for being here?'

'Just said she was passing and had a bit of time to kill. Thought she'd drop in for a cup of coffee. As I said, I just think she was being nosy.'

'Presumably you invited her in. How did you get on?'

'If you really want to know, I don't think I'll ever get on with Fiona. To be honest, Martin, I don't like her much. In fact, that's an understatement. I actually find her pretty obnoxious. Dog felt the same way.'

'What do you mean?'

'I think if I hadn't reined him in he might have had a go at her.'

'Jesus, Beth, I told you from the start that the animal's fucking dangerous. The last thing we need is somebody suing us for keeping a dangerous dog.'

'OK, I take your point,' said Beth, hoping to calm the situation. 'I'll be sure to watch him more carefully in the future. But it's strange. I don't understand why he takes against some and not others. He was fine with the vet, he's fine with the postman and he's fine with any of the delivery people who come to the door. And he's been as good as gold the few times James has dropped by. Apart from that first encounter with you, Fiona's the only other person to whom he's shown any aggression whatsoever. I just can't understand it.'

'Well, if anything does happen don't say I didn't warn you,' Martin said harshly before turning to go and change out of his business suit. As usual, the subject of Dog hadn't failed to cause disharmony.

***

A couple of days later, rushing to meet Martin for lunch, Beth leant in to retrieve her bag which she'd left in the footwell of the passenger seat of the car. Being in such a hurry, she carelessly misjudged the height of the car door as she went to slam it closed, resulting in a painful knock to her jaw as she closed it. Ignoring the smarting pain, and berating herself as a clumsy idiot, she turned and walked into Martin's office, hoping he wouldn't be upset that she was ten minutes late. She'd got carried away with her research into the history of Hill House and had forgotten to keep an eye on the time. Their lunch together would now be a bit shorter than usual.

Bridget was in her place at reception, ready to welcome callers. She looked up and smiled when she saw Beth but then exclaimed, 'What's happened to your face?'

'Oh, that,' answered Beth, rubbing her jaw. 'Does it show?'

'Does it show? It looks blinking painful to me. What have you done?'

'Whacked myself with the car door. Stupid of me, I know. I seem to be becoming accident prone.'

Just then, Martin emerged from his office and started to usher Beth out saying, 'I need to be back by two o'clock, so we'd better get going.' He hadn't seemed to notice the bruise that was now beginning to form. Or if he did, he didn't comment.

Bridget gave a little wave goodbye, thinking it odd that Martin hadn't seemed curious or concerned when the bruise to Beth's jaw was so obvious.

It was only when they got to the pub that Martin asked what had happened. Beth told him and then brushed it aside, saying it was only a slight knock that would disappear in a day or two.

Settling at a corner table, and having each ordered a ploughman's, time being short, Beth casually asked Martin if this was where he'd taken Fiona to lunch.

'What makes you think I took Fiona to lunch?'

'She told me how you'd taken her out to show your appreciation of her value both in sales and for her help in setting up the office.'

'I didn't take her out to lunch. I took the whole team out to lunch and might have mentioned the excellent sales figures. And that applied to everyone, not just Fiona. You must have got the wrong end of the stick.'

'I didn't, Martin. It's what she implied and what she wanted me to believe. I don't know what her game is, but I get the distinct feeling that she dislikes me so much she's out to cause trouble.'

'For God's sake, Beth. I have enough animosity to deal with in the office without my wife stirring it up as well.'

Beth dropped the subject, but the atmosphere had taken a downturn and her hopes of a pleasant lunch were again, ruined.

Getting into bed that night, Beth had forgotten to remove her pendant, which she'd taken to wearing constantly during the day.

She was shocked when Martin turned to her and said, 'Take that fucking thing off, Beth. I don't like it.'

'Why?' Beth asked. 'You've always admired everything I've made. What's to not like about this particular creation?'

'There's just something about it. It gives me the creeps, if you must know. Maybe it's the combination of black and white, or the design or whatever. Anyway, why do you always have to wear that one when you've got loads of alternatives that you don't seem to bother with these days.' He turned away from her, mumbling, 'The same as you don't seem to bother about me any more.'

Beth was shocked, and more than a little hurt. 'That's just not true, Martin. I don't know how you can say that.'

'Well, I'm saying it, and I'm feeling it. You care more for that lousy animal than you do for me.'

Beth lay awake wondering what to make of his outburst. It was so unlike Martin. It was as though he was going through a personality change. She'd never known him to be needy in the past. Nor had she known him to be so moody. Something was going badly wrong with their relationship and she was at a loss as to how to deal with it.

***

The following morning Martin arrived earlier than usual at the office and was surprised to see that Fiona was already there.

'You're early,' he commented, removing his coat.

'Well, you know what they say, Martin, the early bird and all that.' She smiled at him then got up and moved towards the coffee machine. 'Coffee?' she asked.

'Yes, please. Just the thing,' said Martin, turning towards her. 'By the way, Fiona, I'm surprised you didn't mention your visit to my house the other day.'

'I thought it best not to.'

'Really? Why is that? Surely it was no secret.'

'No, of course not. It's just that it wasn't the pleasant experience I was expecting. I'm sorry to say that Beth wasn't all that welcoming.' Fiona forced herself to look tearful.

'I can't believe that.'

'Oh, I think you can, Martin, when I tell you that that vicious dog of hers almost went for me. And I have to say that Beth wasn't at all sympathetic. In fact, I'd go so far as to say that she was downright unfriendly. And I'd only popped in as I was passing, thinking she'd welcome the company.'

'That's just not like Beth, Fiona.' Martin noticed her distress but resisted the urge to make any move to comfort her, anticipating that any indication of sympathy would be misinterpreted. 'She did mention the dog incident and I'm sorry about that, and glad that Beth had the situation under control, but as for the other, I'm sure you must be misreading the situation.'

'Think what you will, Martin. After all, you're bound to believe your wife and that's fair enough. But if I were you, I'd put my foot down and insist on getting rid of that horrible animal before something awful happens.'

At that moment young Malcolm breezed in, putting an end to the discussion.

Fiona sat back down at her desk, satisfied that she'd sown seeds of doubt about his nice accommodating wife.

Chapter Twenty-Four

Hard as nails, Pickie. Time's done nowt to soften the bastard's soul. He's passed on his cold heart all right. Right down through William and the rest. It's time it was put an end to. And we will. You and me, Pickie. We'll be puttin' an end to it before long. If that one thinks she's goin' to hurt me babbie she's mistaken, eh, Pickie? The lust is in her, just as it was in him. She wants him. And she'll have him. She's not one to take no for an answer. They deserve each other. Blood will out. There's no mistakin' those greedy eyes filled with lechery. The generations haven't dulled the urges. Usin' folk is what she's about. Kin of a sort she might be but she'll not have me mercy. Not now I've seen her. Seen me nasty da in her as clear as though it was yesterday. Whatever pity was once within me is long gone. Taken from me. Bitterness is what's in me now. Our yew has put the spite in me to give me strength. Flesh and blood they might be for the time bein'. But we're stronger than them now, Pickie. You'll see. We'll have our day.

Chapter Twenty-Five

To her astonishment, Beth's research had uncovered that until 1932 Hill House had been owned by a family called Wilshaw. Could this possibly, by some bizarre quirk of fate, be Martin's never-talked-about family? Martin had only known the little that he'd been told over the years by his reluctant family, but the coincidence was too much to ignore and she wondered how it would be possible to find out. Sadly, Martin was an only child who had lost both parents, his mother just three years ago from cancer. The only member of the family left, as far as Beth knew, was an aged aunt who Martin had described, rather unkindly, as ga-ga. And Beth recollected him mentioning that this aunt was confined to a care home somewhere on the south coast.

She now knew that Hill House had at one time been owned by a Thomas Wilshaw, described simply as 'merchant'. He and his wife, Henrietta, had produced only one child. A son, Gregory, who had gone on to marry one Freda Lockwood. Gregory had inherited the property in nineteen eighteen on the death of his father. There was no mention of the death of the mother, Henrietta. Beth could see from the records that in nineteen thirty-two the property was sold to a family called Seaton. There was no further mention of the Wilshaws in the Durham records. This would tally with Martin's story of the family moving away from the area after the loss of the family fortune due to some profligate ancestor. It would also explain, if the family had moved south, why there were no further records of the family locally after that time.

At this point, Beth knew she could only surmise. She obviously couldn't be certain that these particular Wilshaws had any connection to Martin. But if she was right, then the offending ancestor in question must have been Gregory. And after all, Wilshaw didn't appear to be a common name hereabouts, or anywhere else for that matter, as far as she could tell. It would be amazing if, from further research, Beth could enlighten Martin about the mystery of his past. She decided to keep her findings to herself for the time being, not wanting to jump the gun. If she could dig up some sort of proof to substantiate her theory then Martin would surely be over the moon. And he wouldn't be able to accuse her of spending more time on Dog than she did on him.

That evening, Martin surprised Beth by suggesting that they ought to go ahead with the housewarming before the winter really set in. Beth's earlier suggestions to go ahead had up until now been met with reluctance, so now that he'd finally agreed they should get on with it, she was instantly heartened. They made plans over dinner and decided on a Saturday three weeks hence. The guest list was small, Martin's work colleagues plus

James and Chris. That would be only six plus the two of them. Martin left the details to Beth but said he would mention it to everyone in the office the following day. Beth would contact James and Chris. At last, she thought, there would be a social event to look forward to. Even Martin had seemed to lighten up at the prospect. Beth promised to keep Dog locked in the studio for the duration of the party, Martin insisting that the 'bloody animal' couldn't be trusted.

***

The following Saturday morning Beth drove to the retail park on the outskirts of Durham, hoping to find some pretty napkins and candles in preparation for the housewarming. Browsing the homewares department of M&S, her eye was caught by sets of plain linen napkins which would be ideal for her table setting, but she was having difficulty choosing between the muted, soft aqua and the more vibrant bright orange. Feeling a tap on her shoulder, she turned to find Bridget beside her.

'I thought it was you, Beth. Shopping for something special?'

Pleasantries exchanged, Beth explained her dilemma.

'Well, it depends on what sort of impression you want to give,' suggested Bridget. 'Subdued sophistication or bright and cheery.'

'Can't make my mind up, Bridget. I know which ones my sister would go for but I'm dithering.'

'Then, have you time to dither over a coffee? I've got all day to do nothing so time is something I have plenty of.'

They made their way to the café and, once settled, Bridget brought up the subject of the housewarming.

'I'm so looking forward to seeing your house. The only thing I've learnt from Martin is that it's a self-build and was designed exactly to your specifications. I'm expecting it to be pretty wonderful.'

'Well, please don't expect too much in case you're disappointed. I hope you won't be because I actually love it. And you'll meet James Douglas, the architect, at our little get-together. I have to say he did an amazing job and was a joy to work with.' Beth took a sip of her latte then said, 'Changing the subject, are you familiar with Lanchester at all?'

'Not really, but I've been through it a few times and it looks like a very pretty village. Actually, I remember my grandmother telling me about an aunt of hers who had lived and worked there. Apparently, she was some sort of servant in one of the big houses. I think it was called Hill House. I don't know if it still exists.'

Beth couldn't hide her surprise. 'Wow!' she said, 'that's an amazing coincidence, Bridget. I've been trying to research the history of that particular property because I've discovered that the people who owned it up until nineteen thirty-two had the same surname as Martin. I wondered if there could be a connection.'

'Surely Martin would know.'

'I'm afraid not. Apparently, his family didn't like to talk much about the family history, but they did tell him that they had once owned a substantial property somewhere in County Durham. He was told that the family fortune had unfortunately been squandered away by an ancestor. According to Martin, successive generations never quite got over the loss. And it sounds as though there might have been something shameful which caused them to move well away from the area. So, you see, I can't help wondering.'

'I can certainly understand your curiosity. What does Martin think?'

'That's the thing, you see, Bridget. I haven't mentioned it yet. I was hoping to find out more before saying anything. I want it to remain a secret until I can, or cannot as the case may be, substantiate my findings. It would be great to be able to present him with evidence that his family actually originated from Lanchester and now he's returned, like a homing pigeon. Wouldn't that be something!'

'Well, listen. I might be able to help a bit in that respect. I'd planned to pop over to Chester-le-Street to visit my mother tomorrow so I'll ask her what she remembers. She was only in her teens when her Great Aunt Hilda died, but she was very close to her as a child. She might recall some of the tales she was told about her great aunt's time in service, and about the family in general. I'll see what I can find out. And, I tell you what, how about meeting up again next Saturday morning about the same time and we can have another natter. I must say that I'm quite intrigued with what you've told me. My curiosity is now piqued.'

'I'd love that, Bridget. But, better still, why don't you come to the house? Martin always insists on working Saturday mornings and I get so few visitors. Then you'll have the opportunity to see the house without the others around. Your own personal viewing.'

'That would be really lovely, Beth. It's a date then. And I'm pleased to see that that nasty bruise to your face has cleared up.'

'Oh that! I'd forgotten about it. Anyway, it didn't hurt much and the mark only lasted a couple of days.'

***

After Martin's initial enthusiasm about the upcoming social event, when they'd spent such a pleasant evening discussing details, Beth's anticipated improvement in the state of their relationship failed to materialise. She was disappointed that, despite her efforts, Martin had resisted sex, turning his back each night, professing to be too tired or too stressed or, more often than not, giving no explanation at all. They'd made love only once over the last three weeks and that had been less than satisfactory, Martin lacking his usual enthusiasm.

Beth could remember when making love was an almost nightly event, not a once in three weeks event. It wasn't as though she hadn't tried. She felt like she was transforming into the epitome of the perfect fifties housewife, making sure to have the evening meal prepared and herself presentable for her hard-working man's homecoming. Primping had never come naturally to Beth and she wondered what the hell was she doing anyway? Was she so insecure that she felt the need to compete with Fiona? She had no hard evidence that Fiona was the cause of the problem with Martin. But the bloody woman had succeeded in putting doubts into Beth's head about his fidelity. She decided there and then to stop playing the little woman and get back to where she was before her equilibrium had been knocked off balance. It wasn't working anyway, and if Chris knew of the way she'd been behaving, Beth didn't doubt that she'd be on the receiving end of a good dressing down. She smiled at that thought. A dressing down for dressing up.

***

Malcolm liked Mrs Wilshaw, which is why he didn't like the way Fiona acted with Martin. He could see what she was doing, constantly popping into Martin's office on some pretext or other. Standing too close to him. Leaning over him to point out some detail on whatever she was showing him. He thought Martin would be a fool if he let her come between him and Mrs Wilshaw. Malcolm had yet to bring himself to call Mrs Wilshaw by her first name, even though the others did. His mam and dad had brought him up to show respect.

He could tell that both Bridget and Harold had noticed Fiona's behaviour. How could they not? Bridget disapproved of office gossip, but Malcolm noticed the grim look on her face every time Fiona made for Martin's office. When Harold noticed Fiona's behaviour he just seemed to smirk, as if to say 'good luck' to her.

To date, as far as Malcolm could tell, Martin had resisted Fiona's advances, but that morning it appeared that Fiona had stepped up her determination. She'd persuaded Martin to accompany her on a viewing, pleading that she desperately needed his opinion on a huge property she'd managed to secure the contract for. She wasn't sure that the valuation she'd come up with was viable, not having handled anything that substantial before. It would be their biggest sale to date and she needed Martin's input. He'd eventually agreed to accompany her that afternoon. Malcolm couldn't swear to it, but thought he'd heard Bridget mutter, *'Hussy!'* under her breath.

Chapter Twenty-Six

Despite what the mistress had said, Gregory kept comin'. Kept comin', that is, until me condition was such that it was gettin' hard to keep it hidden. He stopped then. Who could I tell, Pickie? I was ruined. Mebbe Mrs Bull might have known of a potion if I'd thought to ask her but I'd left it too late, strappin' meself tight before hidin' me growin' bairn under me pinny. Mrs Bull had noticed though. She looked pityingly at me that day. All she said as she sat down beside me in the back room of the laundry was 'Was it Master Gregory?' I cried then and could only nod me head in shame. But the shame wasn't mine, was it? It was his. I knew Mrs Bull had no choice but to go to the mistress. I think she believed I'd be treated with some compassion. The compassion amounted to a purse to me da and me dismissal. I never learnt how much the mistress thought me and me bairn were worth. Mrs Bull drove me home in the cart and I cried all the way. As she handed over the purse she'd been given, I remember her saying to da that he shouldn't think badly of me. 'Your Bessie's not at fault in this, Mr Ellis', she said. But she didn't know me da. He could come across as nice as ninepence when it suited him. I think he was glad of what happened to me. It proved him right in his dirty mind. I was nowt but a bad'un as far as he was concerned. He had to tell himself that to make himself feel better about his usin' of me. And he was greedy for the money. When Mrs Bull took her leave he dragged me inside and gave me a batterin'. It didn't come as a shock. It was only to be expected. He called me terrible names, Pickie. Names I can't bear to repeat even after lyin' here all this time. He beat me so hard I thought me bairn wouldn't be able to survive. But she did. And me brother'd been born by that time. Me fully formed brother. Two perfect legs and everythin' else in the right place. Da doted on William and I was set to the scrubbin' of the house and all the filthy hard work of the yard. Ma would screech at me and call me a lazy good-for-nothin' when I wearied with the growin' of me babbie. And me foot made me clumsy. They had me toilin' right up 'til me time, and they had to call on Missus Batson to see me through the delivery. I tell you, Pickie, I wouldn't've got through that day without her. And me wee bairn was perfect with her black hair, just like mine. No deformities. I was glad then. Glad that she had my hair and not the wishy-washy hair of Gregory. And she was so perfectly made. I wish you could have seen her. I tell you, Pickie, she was beautiful. Really beautiful.

Chapter Twenty-Seven

Martin was uncomfortable having Fiona beside him in the passenger seat. He was finding their close proximity and her perfume a little too intoxicating. His eyes kept wandering to her stockinged thighs where she'd allowed her skirt to ride up, and his attempts at small talk weren't managing to distract him from lustful thoughts. There was no doubt that there was some sort of electrical charge developing between them and he wondered if he'd be able to resist if she made a move. Feeling a stirring down below, he was beginning to have his doubts. And would it be such a bad thing anyway? Life at home wasn't exactly a bowl of fucking cherries at the moment.

It wasn't that Beth wasn't making an effort, it was that, for some reason, he was unable to reciprocate. Beth was changing, and he didn't like the person she was turning into. She'd always been so accommodating in the past. Gone along with whatever he wanted. She seemed to be becoming more forceful. More argumentative.

He'd had the odd fling a couple of times before and he'd managed to get away with it, thank God. Both times it had been at conferences when he'd had too much to drink. Each time they'd gone their separate ways and that was that. No come-back. Fiona was a totally different proposition. It would be fucking dangerous. Maybe that was where the attraction lay. The danger. The excitement. He forced himself to concentrate on the road.

Reaching their destination, even though Fiona had shown Martin the details of the property, it hadn't really prepared him for the magnificence of the building. It was an impressive and enormous Victorian mansion set in several acres of once manicured grounds, now requiring attention. It was no wonder that Fiona needed a second opinion. They got out of the car and Fiona extracted a large bunch of keys from her bag. He followed her inside, noting the long legs and the sway of the hips as she walked ahead of him.

Later, he berated himself for his weakness. It had happened so quickly. So easily. One minute they were surveying the huge kitchen, the next Fiona was perched on the big old pine table with her legs apart, revealing the tops of the stockings where they fell just short of the black lacy underwear. Martin thought afterwards that he'd have defied any red-blooded man to resist.

Shit, he thought as he drove home that evening, remembering the smug, satisfied look on Fiona's face as they'd driven back to the office. He just hoped none of the others had noticed the change. Unlike Beth, Martin didn't rate monogamy all that highly on the agenda, but it was one thing to have a brief encounter with a stranger and another to bugger about so close to home. The worst thing was that he doubted Fiona would settle for a one-off. He'd take her aside tomorrow and make sure she understood that it couldn't happen again.

***

Bridget turned up on Saturday morning as arranged, smiling and eager to look over the house and to tell Beth what she'd been able to find out about Hill House. Beth had heard the car pull into the drive and went out to greet her, forgetting that Dog was outside. She had a brief moment of panic, remembering Dog's behaviour when Fiona had visited. Her fears turned out to be groundless. As Bridget approached the door, Dog came sauntering around the corner and gently licked the fist that Bridget held out to let him smell.

'So you're the vicious beast I've been hearing about,' she said, stroking Dog's shaggy coat. 'I think you've been unjustly accused.'

Beth laughed with relief and led Bridget into the hall and up the stairs. Bridget was immediately drawn to the huge glass wall, taking in the beauty of the surrounding landscape.

'What an absolutely glorious view,' she said, 'as well as a truly amazing house. I have to admit, Beth, I didn't expect it to be so spectacular. Congratulations, not only on the fabulous design but on the location as well.'

'Well, you can congratulate James Douglas when you meet him, Bridget. He's the one who should have the credit. I'd never have been able to achieve this without his invaluable help.'

Beth had been busy in the kitchen in anticipation of Bridget's visit and had baked both scones and a tasty looking carrot cake complete with cream cheese topping. They chatted in the kitchen as she made the coffee and then they moved into the lounge, taking seats either side of the generously sized coffee table.

'I've been so looking forward to this visit, Beth, not least because I'm keen to tell you what I've found out from my mother about Hill House. My mother might be in her late eighties but she's still as sharp as they come. In fact, her memory's far better than mine, as she so often reminds me,' said Bridget, laughing. 'Anyway, she proved the point when she began telling me all that she remembered from way back to the years spent with her aunt and, believe me, her powers of recollection never cease to amaze me.'

Beth leant forward in her chair, eager to hear everything that Bridget had to tell her about Hill House and its occupants. 'I'm all ears, Bridget. It's so good of you to go to so much trouble.'

'Oh, it was no trouble. My mother's in her element when asked to reminisce about Aunt Hilda. And, in fact, I think I'm probably just as keen on what she had to say as you must be to hear it. I have to say, I found it all absolutely fascinating, so here goes.

'After Great Aunt Hilda retired, she came to live with my grandmother. My mother's family, that is, where she lived for the rest of her days, rest her soul. Mother was a little girl of seven when Hilda came to live with them and had just turned fourteen when Hilda died, so they spent quite a lot of time together. I think my mother loved her Aunt Hilda almost as much as she did her own mother, and she was fascinated by the goings on at Hill House. Hilda had gone to work there as a laundry maid after her husband of only a few years, Albert Bull, a kind man by all accounts, was tragically killed in a mining accident. Sadly, she never remarried and she remained childless. Maybe that's why when she came to live with my grandparents she doted on my mother, and vice versa. Gradually, having started as a lowly laundry maid, due to her hard work and diligence, she was eventually put in charge when the woman who held that position retired. Aunt Hilda, having proven herself to be a competent needlewoman, was eventually made responsible for the mending of the linen as well as overseeing the laundry. As you can imagine, in a house that size, she had her work cut out for her. According to my mother there were never less than three other laundry maids that she had to keep her eyes on. She was quite scathing about the idleness of some of them, although she said that she always gave praise where praise was due.'

Bridget paused and took a sip of her coffee. 'Now then, I seem to be getting away from the point. You were quite right about the son, Gregory, being responsible for the loss of the Wilshaw's fortune which, my mother tells me, was quite substantial when the estate was passed to him on the death of his father. So that would fit with what you've told me about Martin's family. It's got me pretty convinced, anyway.'

'Wow! That's brilliant, Bridget. Mind you, I'm not sure how Martin will react when I tell him what we've found out.' Beth laughed. 'Will he be pleased to find out that his family once lived in that huge house, or will he be disappointed that this Gregory character lost the family fortune?'

'Well, if nothing else, it'll make a good dinner party tale for him to tell. It's strange, isn't it? It's almost as if fate pulled him back here.'

'Perhaps only to mourn what might have been,' said Beth. 'Especially when he takes a look at Hill House. No wonder his mother was disgruntled.'

'Oh, and there's something else,' said Bridget, rooting around in her bag. 'I almost forgot. I've got something here I want to show you. My mother's held on to it ever since her aunt Hilda passed on. And it's rather beautiful.'

Bridget pulled an envelope from her bag and passed it to Beth. Inside, carefully wrapped in tissue paper, was a little white linen handkerchief, exquisitely embroidered with delicate sprigs of lavender and pretty primroses. The colours were as fresh as though it were made yesterday. Holding it, Beth experienced a sudden urge to weep. For some reason, as she handled it, she was overcome with overwhelming sadness. Feeling a little foolish, and hoping to hide her emotion from Bridget, she continued to inspect the delicate needlework, noticing the initials HB in one corner. Looking up, she said, 'HB? That's the work of your mother's Great Aunt Hilda then?'

'No, actually. There's a tragic little story attached to that handkerchief, which takes me back to the Wilshaws, and to Gregory in particular. When you hear it, you might well think there was some sort of divine retribution in the eventual loss of the family estate.'

'This is all really fascinating, Bridget. But, before you go on, 'I think more coffee is called for, don't you?' said Beth.

'Definitely. If I'm not taking up too much of your time.'

'God, no, Bridget. I'm loving your company and can't wait to hear the history of the little hankie.'

'Good. And while you're making the coffee I'll tuck into this delicious looking carrot cake,' Bridget said, taking a generous slice and putting it on her plate. 'I'm sure I'll have cause to regret my sweet tooth in the future, but for the time being I'll enjoy the self-indulgence.'

Chapter Twenty-Eight

Do you see her, Pickie? She's got the same heart as me kind Mrs. Bull. The same love in her that was shown to me by her kin. And look, she's showin' me babbie the hankie I made.

Chapter Twenty-Nine

Once settled with a fresh cup of coffee, Bridget continued with her tale.

'Great Aunt Hilda told my mother about a young girl who came to work in the laundry. Apparently, she was a pretty little thing, the most striking thing about her being her thick, black wavy hair, not unlike yours, I imagine. Well, I suppose that wasn't the most striking thing about her actually because the girl had something wrong with one of her feet. Aunt Hilda had said that in those days it was called 'club foot'. I don't know what the correct medical term would be today. The girl's name was Bessie Ellis and she was a timid little thing by all accounts. Just gone fourteen when she came to work at Hill House. Despite her disability, she worked as hard, if not harder than the other laundry maids. Aunt Hilda sort of took her under her wing and grew quite fond of her. This cake is delicious, by the way.' Bridget mopped up the crumbs before carrying on. 'Anyway, after a while, Hilda noticed that the other women were taking advantage of young Bessie, leaving her to carry out most of the hardest work. Sort of bullied her, in a way. It always seemed to be Bessie who she'd find turning the mangle or pulling heavy steaming sheets out of the boiler with the tongs while the others took it a bit easier. So Hilda, who wasn't always around to supervise the division of labour, took it upon herself to try the girl out on mending the linen. That way, young Bessie would be able to sit for a while each day fixing frayed hems on the sheets and whatnot. The girl was a quick learner and apparently proved to be surprisingly deft with a needle. I know I'm being a bit long-winded here, but the story is really quite fascinating, and when I tell you what happened you'll get an idea of the nature of the Wilshaw family at that time.'

'Bridget, I'm thoroughly fascinated by anything you can tell me about them, especially as it's looking likely that anything I learn could possibly be part of Martin's family history. I'm all ears and dying to hear the rest of the story about this Bessie Ellis.' Beth hadn't put down the little hankie and was still gently moving her fingers over the beautiful needlework as Bridget continued.

'It seems that, after a bit of practise, young Bessie's stitching, even on the most basic tasks, was so fine that Hilda moved her on to more intricate work, testing her out on mending any bits of embroidery on the napkins which were damaged. As you can imagine, a lot of napkins were used in a house that size and the mistress was strict about the condition of the family initials being in good order. Hilda was so impressed with Bessie's work that eventually she brought it to the attention of the mistress, Henrietta. It wasn't long before Bessie was put to work on Henrietta's wardrobe, her job being to check daily on any repairs, a task she apparently carried out with great skill. As a consequence, Hilda saw less and less of Bessie but she was glad that the girl didn't have to spend her time slaving away in the steaming laundry room. Still, when there was no work to be done for Henrietta, Bessie would come down and help Hilda out with the less glamorous everyday laundry mending, happy to chat about the work upstairs, describing the beautiful gowns she got to handle.

Hilda was one of the few servants who didn't live in, earning just enough to be able to carry on renting the tiny property that she and Albert had lived in during their short marriage. One day young Bessie was excited to tell Hilda that she'd been given her own room in the attic after one of the older girls had left to get married. Up 'til that time she'd had to share a room with three other servants, so when the room became available the mistress, in appreciation no doubt, had allocated it to young Bessie.'

'So, Henrietta must have valued Bessie quite highly, then,' Beth commented.

'I suppose so. But when I tell you what happened next, it may have been the worst thing that could have happened to the girl. All was well for several months but then Hilda noticed that Bessie gradually became morose, which wasn't like her. No amount of quizzing could get Bessie to open up about what was troubling her and Hilda became increasingly concerned. Being a canny sort, Hilda had an inkling of what the problem was but hoped she was wrong. Nevertheless, her worst fears were confirmed when she came across Bessie one afternoon crying her eyes out in the little back room of the laundry where the clean linen that was waiting to be taken upstairs was stored. When telling the story to my mother, Hilda, who nobody had ever heard uttering even the mildest of swear words, said 'I was so bloody angry, pet, I could have murdered the bastard there and then.'

'What was the problem?'

'The poor girl was pregnant. Barely sixteen and pregnant. Can you imagine? Anyway, putting her arms around Bessie to try to comfort her, Hilda guessed immediately who the culprit was. She quietly whispered, "Was it Gregory?" to which the girl just nodded and carried on sobbing. It was early in the afternoon, and realising that Bessie was in no state to carry on working that day, Hilda took her up to her little attic room with a cup of warm milk and put her to bed. She then went and told the mistress that Bessie had come down with a stomach upset. Hilda knew she couldn't do anything for Bessie in the long run but, while she remained at Hill House, she'd do her utmost to comfort the poor girl.'

'A pretty awful character from the start then, this Gregory! And it seems he didn't change as time went by either, resulting in the squandering of his inheritance. So, what happened to poor Bessie?'

'When her condition became apparent, she was sent packing, even though she was carrying Gregory's child. I think the Wilshaws paid enough bribe money to Bessie's family to persuade them to forget who the father was. That's the sort of family they were, Beth.'

'What happened to her after that? Did Hilda keep in touch with Bessie after she left?' Beth was still holding on to the little hankie, desperately hoping there was more to tell, now more interested in the tale of Bessie than in the Wilshaws' downfall.

'She did for a little while. At least she tried, but was never able to see Bessie without her parents hovering, and was never invited into the house, or hovel, as Hilda put it. She visited a few times but it was a couple of weeks after the baby was born that she learnt the sorry story. It seems the baby, a girl, was immediately put into an orphanage. Hilda never found out which one. By this time Bessie's mother had also given birth. A boy. A brother to Bessie. Hilda was upset seeing how sad Bessie was. Can you imagine what it would be like to have your own baby taken away only to have to live in the same house as another? Hilda gave up trying to visit Bessie after a while. The girl had become uncommunicative, and Hilda was never allowed to be alone with her anyway. She was always kept standing outside, either the mother or father lingering within earshot. Eventually Hilda gave up.'

'So your Aunt Hilda never found out what happened to Bessie after that?'

'Well, the story doesn't quite end there. Several years went by and one day there was a knock on the door to the laundry. Every few weeks or so a young tinker lad would visit Hill House to make sure the knives and other utensils were kept sharp. He'd carry on his work outside in the yard, but on this one day, before he started work, he asked to speak to Mrs Bull, refusing to tell anyone else what he wanted. When Hilda came to the door he reached into his inside pocket and pulled out that little hankie you're holding, saying that it was a present from Bessie. It was from him that Hilda learnt that Bessie was no longer at home with her parents. She was now living on a farm a few miles away, housekeeping for a widower called Sadler. Bessie had apparently asked the young man to tell Hilda that she'd never forgotten the kindness Mrs Bull had shown her so she'd made the hankie for her and he was to make sure she got it. Hilda was so moved that she said she almost broke down in tears there and then. "Is she happy, little Bessie?" she asked the lad. "I wouldn't say that, missus," he answered. "I know I shouldn't speak out of turn, but I'm telling you Sadler's not an easy man." Hilda was obviously upset to hear that and, having got the address from him, she asked him to tell Bessie that she was overjoyed with the present and that she'd go and thank Bessie in person as soon as she got the chance.'

Chapter Thirty

I don't know where they took her on that third day. And they never told me. But see, Pickie, she survived. Was mebbe even loved. And she must have bore a babbie who, in turn, bore a babbie. It was meant to be. We were laid where we were for a purpose. Our tree welcomed us. Clasped and preserved us. Held us. Showed us we have a purpose. And now the time's right and she's waked us to carry out the amends we have to make. Me and you have things to fix.

I didn't weep and wail when me da drove off with her in the cart, Pickie. Why would I? Why would I want me beautiful bairn to be anywhere near me rotten family? Growin' up belittled and used like I was. And mebbe worse to come in time. I was undeservin' of the way they treated me. Why would I want that for me innocent bairn? I was of the mind that wherever she'd gone had to be better than bein' in that godless house. As far as I was concerned, the further away the better. You see, Pickie, I wasn't like them. I let her go in the hope she'd find the love I never had. Me ma and da hung onto me even though they'd no love for me from the start. I think Da expected a boy but he got me instead. I wasn't just a girl, I was a girl with a deformity. An

143

embarrassment. They didn't bother takin' me to the doctor to see if I could be fixed. Likely didn't see the point of spendin' money on a useless girl. It's a wonder they held on to me at all. Almost as soon as I was able to walk, or hobble, they set me to chores. I had to grow up quick, Pickie. And until I was sent to Hill House, I thought that was just how life was for everybody. I knew no other. How could I? Tucked away on the farm as though I was an abomination to be hidden. Not seein' how other folks lived. Why would I want that for me beautiful babbie?

Chapter Thirty-One

'This is so fascinating, Bridget. There's more, I hope.'

'Not much, I'm afraid. It was a few weeks before Hilda was able to make the journey to the Sadler farm and when she got there she found Bessie had gone. All she managed to get out of the farmer, a big brute of a man, according to Hilda, was that she'd buggered off with that tinker lad. And that was that, I'm afraid. Hilda never heard of Bessie again and the young tinker didn't come back either to clear up the mystery. Another man had taken his place, and he told Hilda that Billy Clarke — Hilda hadn't known his name until now — had gone and got himself a job in the shipyards on Tyneside and passed his tools on. So it seemed that the farmer must have been right about where Bessie had gone. But Hilda never forgot Bessie and she always treasured that little hankie which, I suppose, is why my mother holds onto it.'

***

Chris arrived the day before the party and insisted on contributing by providing two crates of wine, by her own admission being hopeless in the kitchen and therefore of little use in that respect. It had been decided that, with only eight of them, a sit-down meal would be preferable to a buffet, so Beth spent most of that day doing as much prior preparation as possible. She was going all out to make it a special affair and wanted everything to be perfect. Chris, true to form, sat on the kitchen stool making inroads into a bottle of chilled Pinot Grigio.

'So that's why you insisted on two crates,' commented Beth, nodding at the glass in Chris's hand.

'Of course. Hopefully your guests will be of the abstemious sort and there'll be plenty left for Sunday.'

'Knowing you, Chris, there might not be any left for tomorrow.'

'True. We've got tonight to get through yet. Have you done enough now? Isn't it time you relaxed and helped me finish off this bottle? And I want to hear all about what's been going on between you and Martin. Have things improved?'

Beth washed her hands, accepted the proffered glass of wine and they moved into the lounge.

'Come on. Spill the beans,' demanded Chris.

'Things are still the same, Chris. If anything, it seems to be getting worse. And before you ask, our sex life is almost non-existent.'

'Whoa! That's not good, Beth. The longer that goes on, the further away from each other you'll drift.'

'Well, I promise you, it's not for lack of trying on my part. Martin just seems to have completely lost

146

interest. But please don't say anything. He wouldn't thank me for discussing our sex life, even with you.'

'Of course I won't say anything. You know me better than that. And you really have no idea what the problem is? Presumably you've given it lots of thought.'

'I've hardly been able to think of anything else. The move to Durham seems to have been the catalyst. Maybe it's the house, or the dog, or the job. I just can't put my finger on it. Maybe it's me that's changing and he doesn't like it. I've even tried playing the perfect little housewife.'

'In what way?'

'Oh, you know, the fifties ideal. Cooking, cleaning, making sure dinner's ready, tarting myself up before he walks in the door. That sort of thing. Pathetic, isn't it.'

'Too right it is and you can bloody well stop doing that right now. I won't put up with having a dogsbody for a sister.'

Chris put her arms around Beth and held her. 'What you need is a top-up. And tomorrow morning I think a bit of retail therapy is called for. Something to cheer you up. And don't tell me you won't have the time. Most of the food's already prepared and you need to get yourself equally prepared. I presume that the flirtatious bitch we saw in the restaurant will be in attendance?'

'You think Martin's having an affair, don't you?'

'No, I don't, Beth, but with a man-eater like her on the scene, it might be time for you to remind both Martin and yourself of the sexy, beautiful woman he married.

147

Never mind the pandering to his bloody ego slaving away in the kitchen, I think a bit of glamour is called for. And, before you say it, I'm not suggesting this is for him, but to make *you* feel good. Whatever's going on in Martin's head, it seems to me that you've been doing everything you can to try to solve the problem. It's now down to him and it's time for you to think about yourself. Anyway, I'm not taking no for an answer, even if I have to cook tomorrow night's dinner myself.'

Beth laughed. 'As if,' she said. 'I've tasted your offerings and unless it's a take-away, they're barely edible. But, okay. It's a deal. We'll go shopping but you're not forcing me into some seductive, unsuitable figure-hugging number just to try to compete with Fiona.'

'We'll see,' laughed Chris.

***

Martin arrived home that evening with a bunch of red roses and a large box of hand-made chocolates.

Chris greeted him with a peck on the cheek and a 'Who's been a naughty boy then! Guilty conscience Martin?'

'Can't a man buy his wife flowers for no particular reason other than that he wanted to? And hello to you as well, Chris.' He returned the peck. 'I see you've been at it already,' noting the glass of wine in her hand. 'I've obviously got some catching up to do.'

Beth came in from the kitchen and handed Martin a glass of his favourite red. 'They're absolutely gorgeous, Martin,' she said, taking the flowers from him. 'Thank you. I'd better get them into water before we do anything else.'

'Just a thank you, darling, in appreciation of all the effort I know you're putting into this party to make it a success,' he called after her.

Beth and Chris exchanged looks, both wondering what had brought on Martin's sudden lightening of mood.

***

The following morning Beth and Chris drove into Newcastle for the planned shopping trip. Chris tried to persuade Beth into what were, in Beth's opinion, several inappropriate, slinky dresses in which she felt exposed and uncomfortable.

'You need to be more adventurous, sis,' Chris said. 'Give that Fiona woman a run for her money. I wish you realised just how beautiful you are. Here's me having to spend a fortune on hair salons, the search for clothes which disguise my big clumsy bones and generally doll myself up to the nines to get a look in. And there's you with your beautiful dark hair and svelte figure which you always seem to want to hide. I don't understand it.'

Eventually, having rejected all of Chris's recommendations, Beth finally settled on her own choice, and Chris had to admit that Beth looked stunning in the simple and elegant, cornflower-blue, silk, knee-length shift. Afterwards, foregoing lunch because of the limited time available, they settled on takeaway coffees which they drank sitting on the steps beneath Grey's Monument before making their way home. The guests were due to arrive at seven thirty and there was still a bit to do.

***

The afternoon was spent in a flurry of activity, Beth working away in the kitchen while Chris sipped wine and kept her sister amused with hilarious updates of her life in the world of public relations and her most recent sexual conquests. Despite the laughter, Beth sensed a touch of loneliness in her sister. She wondered if Chris would ever find a permanent partner. She hoped so.

Just after seven thirty Chris answered the door to James, the first to arrive and bearing a large terracotta plant pot which he explained was already planted with tulip bulbs. He also produced a bottle of Möet & Chandon, already chilled.

Chris's first glance at the ruggedly handsome face and friendly, relaxed attitude, had the effect of her moving instantly into flirtatious mode. She took James by the arm while divesting him of the champagne. 'A man after my own heart,' she said, kissing him on the cheek. 'I'm Beth's little, but bigger sister, Chris. And you are?'

'James.'

'Ah, the famous architect. No Mrs James?'

'Not for a while. Just me, I'm afraid.'

'I've been so eager to meet you James,' Chris cooed. 'Beth's been waxing lyrical about your talents, the proof of which we're standing in, of course.'

'Er, shouldn't we make our way up?' suggested James, feeling a little out of his depth having been greeted by this forceful but attractive woman. He would never have guessed that she and Beth were sisters.

Chris gave a dramatic sigh. 'I suppose we must,' and she sashayed ahead of him up the stairs.

Fiona was the next to arrive, dressed in a slinky, off-the-shoulder little black number, determined to outshine Beth, not that she thought that presented much of a challenge. She was disappointed when the door opened and she was met by an utterly transformed Beth. Fiona noted the elegant dress which she immediately recognised as being in the upper price range. Beth was looking a bit too classy for her liking. She almost wished she'd worn something a bit less revealing than the skin-tight, low-necked black number she'd decided on.

Without so much as a hello, Fiona launched straight into, 'You've got that dog safely locked away, I hope.' She was holding on to a bottle of Bollinger.

'Glad you could make it,' said Beth, feeling her hackles rise as she forced a smile.

Fiona moved past Beth and headed up the stairs. On entering the lounge, she made straight for Martin, kissed him on the cheek and proffered the bottle.

'I thought we should all start with something a bit special,' she quietly whispered in his ear.

The whisper wasn't quiet enough to escape Chris's ears. 'You're too late I'm afraid, er, what was your name again?'

'Fiona,' said Martin, sensing the animosity.

'We've already started on something very special, kindly provided by James here. Have you met James, Fiona?' Chris took hold of James's arm as if to say, *Hands off.*

Martin was already feeling uncomfortable and was beginning to wish they hadn't bothered with a get-together at all. The doorbell rang and he was grateful to have something to do. 'I'll get it,' he shouted, hoping to deter Chris or Beth from making their way down to greet the next guest.

Harold, Bridget and Malcolm all arrived together, Malcolm having volunteered to act as chauffeur. Following several unpleasant incidents in his teens he'd decided early on that he didn't much care for alcohol or, rather, it didn't much care for him.

From the moment he arrived Harold had difficulty taking his eyes off Beth, dressed as she was, the vibrant blue of the dress contrasting perfectly with her black hair and pale skin. He thought the addition of the unusual pendant was unnecessary and, for some reason he couldn't fathom, rather distasteful.

Beth took young Malcolm under her wing, noting his shyness. He was gazing around as though overawed by his surroundings.

Bridget, eagle-eyed as usual, hadn't failed to notice Martin's discomfort at being the sole recipient of Fiona's attention. While the others mingled and got to know each other, Fiona had cornered Martin and seemed determined to hang on to him. Chris caught Bridget's look of disgust and moved over to her. 'That woman has no shame,' Chris whispered, recognising in Bridget a kindred spirit.

'Time to rescue him, I think,' smiled Bridget and by tacit mutual consent they both moved in to draw Martin away.

With everyone becoming more relaxed after a couple of glasses of champagne, Beth declared that they should take their seats at the table otherwise dinner would spoil. Not wishing the evening to be too formal, Beth had decided against place names and allowed everyone to choose their own seats. Fiona was out-manoeuvred by Bridget and Chris who beat her to the seats either side of Martin. Fiona did the next best thing and sat immediately opposite him in order to be within foot-fiddling distance, and where Martin would hopefully be unable to tear his eyes away from her cleavage.

Chapter Thirty-Two

See, Pickie. They're all here. Ripe for the pickin'. She's worked her magic for us. She's hungered long enough and she's got us ready. The shameless woman in black actin' so high and mighty. Upsettin' me bonnie. She's me filthy da, all right. I told you that, didn't I. When she came here that first time and you frighted her. I love you, Pickie. And you love me. Together we'll carry out our work.

With me own bairn gone I had to watch ma and da dotin' on William. Smilin' and cooin' and slobberin' over him while I was set to the graft all over again. I don't ever remember her smilin' and cooin' over me. They never gave me no rest, Pickie. Me foot would ache from standin' at the sink washin' and scrubbin', and me arms would hurt from the pumpin' of the water. I did everythin' I was told to do, and God help me if what I did wasn't to their likin'. Neither Da or Ma held back the clouts when they got it in mind. I was their skivvy, Pickie. I was their skivvy right up until Bertram Sadler, the farmer that Da rented the land from got me.

Chapter Thirty-Three

Martin was uncomfortable sitting opposite Fiona and couldn't decide whether having to look at her was better or worse than having her beside him. He was having difficulty controlling the stirring in his loins. He was sure the bloody woman knew the effect she was having on him. The constant attention she was giving him was going to be noticed and that was the last fucking thing he wanted. He cursed himself for his weakness. Did she have to make it so bloody obvious! If he'd had to succumb, he could have at least had the sense to wait until after the fucking party. And she was drinking too much. God knows what she'd let slip.

Everyone but Fiona complimented Beth on her goat's cheese and sun-dried tomato tartlets. For the main course, Beth had played it safe with a rich beef bourgignon, served with buttery mash and green vegetables. Apart from Malcolm, who had insisted he was happy with spring water, everyone was getting stuck into the wine, the company becoming jollier as a consequence.

Moving in and out of the kitchen, clearing plates and seeing to the next course, with Bridget helping, Beth was growing increasingly uneasy with the unwanted attention she was getting from Harold. She'd been aware of him ogling her for most of the evening, and she was also aware of young Malcolm watching Harold with what she correctly surmised was disapproval. She hoped Malcolm didn't think she was giving Harold any encouragement. She wouldn't want him to get the wrong idea. She was also aware that Harold was knocking back the wine more quickly than anyone else. She blushed as Harold commented loudly, 'That's a beautiful wife you have there, Martin, you lucky sod.'

Martin simply agreed with a nod of the head, smiling at Harold, aware that the drink was getting the better of him.

Chris noted the sour look on Fiona's face and concluded that Fiona was put out by Harold's comment, being in a position where, for once, she wasn't the centre of attention.

Beth had just finished serving up the main course and had sat down when Fiona excused herself, saying she needed to visit the 'little girls' room.'

Chris and Bridget exchanged looks before Chris piped up, 'It's not exclusively for little girls, Fiona. Little boys and grown-ups are also allowed, just to make things clear to everyone here.'

Malcolm coughed as Fiona stormed her way out of the room and across the landing. 'You just couldn't help yourself, could you,' Bridget whispered to Chris. Chris simply smiled and shook her head.

***

Fiona was fuming. How dare that smug bitch humiliate her like that! She leaned over the sink and looked up at her angry red face in the mirror. She'd need time to get herself together before going back to the table, picturing them sitting sniggering at her expense. On a whim, she decided that, as she wasn't yet sufficiently got together to go back and sit across from that snide fat cow, she might as well have a quick snoop around.

Fiona quietly left the bathroom and crept along the landing. On glancing into the first room she came to, and seeing the disarray and scattering of only women's paraphernalia, it was obvious to her that it must be the guest room. She moved on to the next door and went in. If anyone came to look for her she'd just say she became disoriented and went the wrong way. A lame excuse, but what the hell! She wanted to check out the marital bedroom. The one that Beth would soon be occupying alone if her plans worked out. Martin had been a bit of a challenge at first but she'd won the battle, as she always knew she would. She cast her eye over the spacious room which, unlike the first room she'd gone into, was neat and tidy, the only items on view being Beth's make-up and perfume on the dressing table and a man's dressing gown slung over the bottom of the bed. She picked it up and held it to her face, breathing in the smell of Martin. It made her want him. Badly. Right now, in the marital bed. It was as she was fantasising about this that she looked up towards the wall of glass doors leading on to the balcony.

She froze as she caught the reflection of someone standing a few feet behind her. At first, she thought it was Beth. But that didn't make sense. Why had she let her hair down? Fiona spun round, ready to make her excuses. What she was confronted with caused her to recoil in horror. The grotesque figure limped towards her, a look of pure hatred and evil intent on a face that was Beth but at the same time wasn't. The black hair on the emaciated woman was long and wild and she was dressed in some sort of shift more suited to a previous century. Fiona could barely move for the fear she felt as the thing advanced, the malice emanating from it palpable. She opened her mouth to scream but her terror was so great that no sound came out. She took a step back as the thing kept limping towards her, Beth's gentle eyes had somehow transformed into pinpoints of loathing and focused directly into Fiona's own. She continued to step back as the inhuman thing continued to move forward, the face and body that was Beth's but wasn't suddenly beginning to shed its flesh. Pieces rotting and falling. Melting. An unbearable stench of decay hit Fiona as the figure, still shuffling towards her, continued to putrefy. Another faltering step backward and Fiona found herself pinned against the central glass door leading out onto the balcony. Unable to drag her eyes away from the grisly sight of the advancing atrocity, she desperately fumbled behind her back, trying to locate a means of getting away, her hands finding nothing that would help. Then, without warning, the glass door seemed to miraculously give way and Fiona found herself outside.

In a brief instant of sanity, she tried telling herself that this couldn't be real. It was a nightmare and she'd soon wake up. She kept on retreating. Her back was now against the rail and the thing was almost touching her. Fiona was finding it difficult to breathe. She tried to turn her head away from the foul stench but found she couldn't. Her face was wet even though she hadn't realised she was crying. With a monumental effort she closed her eyes. When she opened them, the thing would have disappeared. They were still clamped shut as she heard the maniacal cackle. She felt herself being lifted. The cackle turned into a venomous snake-like hiss and Fiona thought she heard the thing utter, *'For you, Da.'* And then she was falling. Fiona found her voice for the last time. Her ear-splitting scream was cut off as she hit the frozen ground. In the last few seconds of consciousness, lying broken and twisted on the cold earth, she looked up. No one was there.

Chapter Thirty-Four

Did you watch that, Da? Are you screamin'? It's my revenge for the spoilin' of me. For the hurt you inflicted. And is my vicious brother William alongside you, and any other wicked bastards you're responsible for? This one's on her way to join you. Comin' to burn with you. She's no better than you. She's a ruiner just as you were. Is Ma there with you? I hope so. Watch. Watch. Watch.

Did you ever consider there'd be a price to pay? It was you who set yourself on the road to her fate. It was you who gave me nowt but fear and pain. And you, Ma. You never gave me any comfort. You made sure William was comforted though. You could all tell, couldn't you! You could tell she was yours. The spittin' image of you, Da. And needin' to satisfy her lust at any cost, just the same. Now she's gone. Her body's all broke up. Just like you broke me. Broke me spirit. Did you see the terror in her eyes? The same sort of terror you saw in mine. Did you enjoy seein' me terrified? Cowerin' under the blanket when I heard your great clumpin' footsteps clatterin' up the stairs. Knowin' there was nowt I could do to make you stop. Did it make you feel powerful? How do you feel now that I'm the one with the power?

Not really powerful enough though for me likin'. Power to put an end to her, yes. But not enough to make her hurt for years and years. It would've been better if I'd been able to eke out her sufferin'. Her death was too easy for her. Do you take any comfort from that? I hope not. Did you treat me bad just because of me club foot? Or would you have treated me just the same if I'd been born whole? I think you would have. There was too much insatiable hunger in you. You made sure me own agony went on and on. Just to satisfy your own lustful cravin's. Do you know how long I've been waitin'? But it's happenin' now. The beginnin' of me healing. I can forget you and Ma and William. You mean nothin'. Nothin' at all. While you all rot in hell, I'm still here, Da. And so is me wee babbie. She's come to me. Just as me carin' yew told me she would.

Chapter Thirty-Five

Just as everyone was wondering what was keeping Fiona, Beth inwardly worrying that her dinner was growing cold, they heard the terrified scream. There was a moment of absolute silence when they all stopped and looked at each other in shock before Martin pushed back his chair and dashed out, closely followed by Malcolm.

'What the hell was that?' Harold slurred drunkenly.

'Attention seeking more than likely,' Chris sneered.

Thinking that Fiona must have fallen in the bathroom, that was the first room Martin and Malcolm headed for, only to find it empty.

'It sounded to me that the scream came from outside,' said Malcolm.

They moved along the corridor and checked the guest bedroom, again finding it empty.

Cold air was coming from the master suite and, on entering, Martin was surprised to find the middle door to the balcony open, the night air causing him to give a slight shiver. A sense of dread came over him as he moved through the door and onto the balcony with Malcolm close on his heels.

'Oh, my God,' Martin gasped, seeing the prone figure of Fiona below. There was a look of utter terror in the glazed eyes which were staring directly up into his own. Martin was transfixed. He found himself rooted to the spot, unable to move.

Malcolm, perhaps because of being completely sober, reacted quickly, turning and rushing down the stairs, shouting to anyone who could hear to ring an ambulance. Martin was still standing looking down in horror when Malcolm arrived at Fiona's side and quickly knelt, feeling her neck for a pulse.

James had come into the bedroom and now stood by Martin, taking in the scene. He pulled out his mobile phone and called the emergency services, hanging on the line while he ran outside to join Malcolm. Beth and Chris, having seen Malcolm rush outside, and not sure of what was happening, ran to Martin's side. His face ashen, he turned to them whispering, 'I think she's dead.'

'Please, God, no,' muttered Beth, not wanting to believe what she'd heard Martin say. What Beth saw, looking down at Fiona's lifeless body, would continue to haunt her forever. Those dead eyes seemed to momentarily come to life, focusing directly into Beth's own. They were accusatory and full of loathing. Beth had no idea why she felt this, or why it should be. She had a sudden urge to be sick and ran into the en-suite where she just made it to the toilet bowl before vomiting. Chris followed her in and gently held back Beth's hair as she heaved.

Bridget, who had followed James and Malcolm down the stairs, knelt down beside the body, looked up at Martin and gently shook her head. Confirmation that there was nothing to be done for the unfortunate Fiona.

All except Harold were gathered in the hall when the ambulance arrived, closely followed by the police. It was soon established that all seven diners had been seated at the table when the incident happened. The police thought it wise to leave the questioning of Harold until the following morning. He was found slumped over the table, seemingly unaware of the drama going on around him.

Fiona's body was eventually taken away in the ambulance and the police finally left at four o'clock in the morning, indicating that although further investigation would be necessary, they didn't suspect foul play at this time.

Chris and Bridget made coffee and they all sat around for the next hour, trying to fathom how it could possibly have happened. Fiona had supposedly simply gone to the toilet, so why had she fallen from the balcony of the master bedroom? There were no suggestions as to the whys and wherefores and therefore no answers to be had.

***

A lot of analysing by all involved could throw no light on what could have happened. Suicide was rejected as a possibility. Everyone who knew Fiona, friends as well as colleagues, were adamant that Fiona just wasn't the type to take her own life, and, besides, she had no reason. Having established beyond any doubt that everybody present on the evening in question had been seated at the table when they heard the scream, the investigation came to a standstill. The police could only conclude that Fiona, somehow, maybe because of the amount of alcohol in her system, had overbalanced. But no one could account for her being where she was when it happened. Why was she in Martin and Beth's bedroom and, more bewildering, what was she doing out on the balcony on such a cold night?

'Having a good old nose around,' suggested Chris sometime later, when discussing it with Beth.

Martin mentally chastened himself for the sense of relief he felt. With Fiona out of the picture, his guilty secret would stay that way. He had no doubt at all that he'd have been too weak to reject further advances from Fiona. And he was pretty bloody certain that she'd intended to make sure Beth eventually found out. Outwardly, he feigned deep sadness at the loss of a valued colleague and friend in such tragic circumstances.

The coroner would eventually record a verdict of accidental death, and the funeral was attended by all but Chris, who had been unable to get the time off work.

Bridget commented afterwards that not many people attended the ceremony, considering Fiona had apparently spent her whole life in the Durham area. 'Makes you think she wasn't very popular,' she whispered to Malcolm.

***

The atmosphere in the office was subdued in the following weeks. Harold and Malcolm shared Fiona's workload, while Martin concentrated on seeking a replacement negotiator.

Young Malcolm stepped up to the challenge with enthusiasm and was more than proving his worth. Martin, unbeknownst to Malcolm, was negotiating with head office to get him a pay rise, predicting that he'd go far in the industry. As for Harold, Martin suspected he had stepped up his drinking. He had smelt alcohol on his breath several times in the mornings when he turned up for work. Added to that was the flushed face and general grumpiness. Martin determined to have a word with him if the situation continued.

Beth was devastated that such a tragedy could occur in their home, and during what should have been a celebration. She didn't kid herself when reflecting on what she'd felt about Fiona, but she couldn't help but feel sadness for the loss of such a young life. After the initial shock, Beth and Martin tried to carry on as normal, each, as though by mutual consent, unwilling to dwell on that fateful evening.

Chapter Thirty-Six

Me babbie'll be all right, Pickie. She's stronger than she looks. I'll wager that the man, the adulterer, the one who doesn't deserve her, is relieved, although he won't show it. He'll be thinkin' now that there's no danger of me bonnie findin' out. He'll get on with his life. For now, Pickie. For now. His come-uppance will be of a different sort. But painful, all the same. He deserves what's comin', Pickie. Are you listenin' Gregory? He'll be burnin' alongside you soon and there's nowt you can do to stop it. Your philanderin' blood runs in his veins. Are you hurtin' in the knowin' of what's to befall? I hope you're lookin' up from Hell and writhin' in agony.

Chapter Thirty-Seven

Beth found some consolation in her work. Her website had been reactivated and, with Christmas almost upon them, she was rushing to fulfil several commissions from both previous buyers as well as some new ones. She spent more and more time in the studio, Dog keeping her company, while Martin spent more time at work. Their relationship hadn't shown any improvement. If anything, it felt to Beth that they were growing even further apart. Martin was constantly complaining, seeming to find fault with everything which in the past he would have shrugged off. If it wasn't something in the office that wasn't going according to plan, then it was something at home. Something that Beth had or hadn't done that annoyed him. Accusing her of neglecting both him and the house.

'I'm busy with orders, Martin,' Beth told him. 'I simply haven't the time to deal with every little bit of housework. Perhaps you could help out once in a while.'

Tonight's complaint was about Dog. Beth hadn't got around to cleaning the muddy paw prints on the hall floor before Martin had arrived home from work. She'd been busy in the kitchen in an effort to cheer him up by spending time cooking him a special dinner.

'You've had that flaming animal up here, haven't you? I can smell him.'

'That's impossible, Martin. I never have and never would bring Dog up here, knowing how much you detest him, despite him never having given you any cause.'

'His bloody presence is enough'

'He's never in your presence. You make sure of that.'

'I'll be happier when he's gone.'

'Gone where?'

'Dog pound, rescue centre, dead. Any of the above.'

'What the hell's got into you lately, Martin? You didn't used to be so cruel. You're almost unrecognisable from the man I married.' With that, before her temper really got the better of her, Beth stormed into their bedroom. Before locking the door behind her she called out, 'Get your own bloody dinner.'

Much later, unable to sleep, she heard Martin come out of the main bathroom and go straight into the guest room. He'd made no attempt to try their bedroom door. Beth eventually cried herself to sleep and didn't get up the next morning until she'd heard Martin leave for work.

***

It was barely three weeks since the party. The first snow of the winter had been falling softly when Martin left the office. Now it had gained momentum. The wipers were working at full capacity but he was still finding it difficult to see. Having lived all of his life in the south-east, Martin hadn't ever experienced weather like this. He supposed he'd get used to it in time. He'd bloody have to. He wished he'd started on the drive home before it had got dark. The wind was now whipping the snow horizontally against the windscreen and Martin had slowed to less than twenty miles an hour in order to cope. At least, he told himself, he was used to going at such a slow speed, given the traffic congestion on the streets of London. Other cars were constantly overtaking him on the long straight road. Locals, no doubt, he thought, used to such fucking dire conditions. He found himself gripping the wheel too tightly. Told himself he needed to try to relax. Subdue the rising panic.

He suddenly remembered there was a layby about a mile ahead. If he could just get there then he'd pull in for a few minutes. Pull in to pull himself together. There it was, just up ahead. Martin heaved a sigh of relief as he killed the engine and rested his head on the steering wheel. He just needed a few minutes before he'd carry on. Christ, he could do with a drink. Just to calm his nerves. He'd been wound up ever since that awful night. And Beth wasn't helping. For some reason, when she wasn't in the studio, she'd now taken to spending the evenings sitting in the armchair crouched over some sort of stitching project. She wasn't interested in making conversation. Which was just as well, he admitted to himself, because all Martin wanted to do these days was plonk himself in front of the telly until bedtime. The days in the office seemed to wear him down and he couldn't be bothered to make an effort at home.

He suddenly wished Fiona hadn't died. At least the excitement of sex for sex's sake with such a willing partner had made him feel alive. More alive than he now felt with Beth. He didn't doubt that were Fiona still around he wouldn't be able to control himself. She'd had that effect on him. A woman who wouldn't take no for an answer. He wouldn't have been able to resist. The anticipated exciting new beginning for himself and Beth was proving to be a bitter disappointment. It wasn't what he'd imagined when he'd agreed to the move north. Everything was falling apart. God, how had he reached the stage where he was sitting in a layby feeling so sorry for himself? He was bloody pathetic.

Martin raised his head and started the engine. The windscreen wipers burst into life, he indicated, then checked his mirror to ensure it was safe to pull out. The traffic had thinned and just as Martin was about to release the handbrake, he thought he saw two figures emerging through the curtain of snow, advancing towards him. He could make out that it appeared to be an inadequately dressed woman along with a dog. The woman looked about the height and build as Beth and

172

she seemed to be limping. 'Jesus,' he muttered to himself. 'Something must be seriously wrong for anyone to be walking along this stretch of road, the houses being so few and far between. And in this weather. The woman must be fucking frozen.' Martin switched the headlamps on to full beam.

'Christ almighty, Beth,' he shouted, opening the car door and running towards the pair. 'What the fuck are you doing? What's happened?'

Beth's hair was wild, and for some reason he couldn't fathom, she was dressed in some sort of thin shift which was flapping around her ankles, revealing bare feet.

When he was within a few feet and about to reach out, he came to an abrupt halt. This wasn't Beth. The woman resembled Beth. And the dog, which was snarling, looked like Dog. But the woman's face, which just a few moments earlier he'd mistaken for Beth, wasn't quite right. Was he hallucinating? Suddenly, Martin drew back in horror as the face seemed to lose substance, pieces of superating flesh beginning to fall away. Melting in front of his eyes; the lips disintegrating, revealing a ghoulish grimace with a missing front tooth; the eyes becoming dead, cavernous black sockets. The hair which a moment ago had been as thick and dark as Beth's was now falling in clumps. He could feel the bile gathering in his throat at the same time as the dog threw back its revolting head, ragged with disintegrating fur and flesh, and emitted a blood-curdling howl.

A brief instant of common sense told Martin that this couldn't be happening. He could feel himself breaking out into a cold sweat. His heart was thumping. He must be going mad. He was ill. He had to somehow get back in his car. Get himself away. But absolute terror was keeping him rooted to the ground. A sinewy arm was slowly raised. A bony finger pointed at him. The thing that wasn't Beth came limping closer. The fear he felt was all-encompassing. He was barely aware of the fact that he'd lost control of his bladder. When the vile, nauseating creature was almost within touching distance the nauseating stench was overwhelming. The dog that wasn't Dog was continuing to snarl, drool dripping from skeletal jaws. Martin had to get away. Away from the grisly mockery of Beth. This abomination. Mustering all the strength left in him he somehow managed to turn and stumble back to the car, not daring to look over his shoulder. He thought he heard the sound of a contented sigh and the words, *For you, Gregory* as he threw himself into the driving seat and, with trembling hands, released the handbrake at the same time as putting his foot flat down on the accelerator. His only thought was to get away. Away from the putrid smell of decay. Away from the grotesque apparition with the accusatory finger.

Without checking, he pulled out. And then Martin was no more. The shocked juggernaut driver had been unable to avoid slamming into the car which had pulled out without any warning.

Chapter Thirty-Eight

He got off lightly, Gregory. Just a few moments of fear. Did you ever consider the months of fear I endured because of your selfish lustin'? I don't think you did. Didn't give me a thought. Even though me condition was of your makin'. And the mistress was no better. There was no way she was goin' to entertain a bastard child. Especially not a bastard child of a cripple. She might have valued me as a seamstress. But not enough. Not enough to show mercy on the innocent servant who was got with bairn by her rotten son. Not enough to secure a decent future for her innocent grandchild. Neither of you bothered to check whether me bairn was a boy or a girl. Whether we lived or died. Just handed money to me greedy da and forgot about us. How many other 'dalliances' did you have, Gregory? How many other girls did you ruin? I'll wager I wasn't the only one. But you must've gone on to marry some unsuspectin' woman and produce at least one legitimate bairn. You must've done because I recognised you in him. Him what's now goin' to be put in the earth to rot away. Him who didn't deserve me lovely bonnie. Him who would have gone on to hurt her. Him who would always succumb to temptation. I couldn't have that, Gregory. I looked at him and saw you. He would've

carried on. And one day me bonnie would've found out.
Better now that she won't. Better he's gone while she's
young enough to get past the sadness. I'm comforted
that she'll never know about his betrayal. But you
should know this, Gregory. Others think badly of him.
I've made sure of that. They believe he was a batterer. I
gave me bonnie the bruises and they didn't go
unnoticed. Mrs Bull and the other one, the one who
looks after me bonnie, won't mourn him. They'll say
nowt. But they'll be secretly relieved, all the same.

Chapter Thirty-Nine

Dog alerted Beth before the clang of the doorbell. She hadn't heard the car pull into the garage so it couldn't be Martin. A visit from Bridget or James or Malcolm at this time of the evening would be unusual. She decided to keep Dog by her side as she went to answer the door, not knowing who to expect. Afterwards, Beth wondered about Dog's behaviour that night. He neither growled nor wagged his tail when she opened that door to the two men in uniform. He simply stood close beside her. As though already knowing. Prepared for her coming sorrow. Ready to bring comfort.

As is so often the case with those who get an unexpected visit from uniformed officers, especially from officers with sombre expressions, Beth knew instinctively that it could only be bad news. She didn't want to hear what they had to say. She simply turned away and walked back up the stairs, Dog at her heels.

The officers were reluctant to leave Beth alone. They could see that the news hadn't yet sunk in. Either that or she was in denial. No hysterics. No weeping and wailing. No wringing of hands. No 'What should I do?' or even 'How did it happen?' They'd experienced such reactions before and knew that with some there was a delay in the willingness to face reality. A non-facing-up. A putting aside until such time as the mind felt able to cope. When asked, she refused to consider the summoning of a grievance counsellor. She wanted no stranger. Yet, Beth knew she needed someone. She was too afraid to be alone. Terrified of the panic that was threatening to erupt, ready to overwhelm her. She couldn't allow that. She had to hold herself together. Stave it off. Wait for a more suitable time. She sat on the edge of the sofa simply staring ahead. Fondling Dog. Saying nothing. The kindly bearers of the unwelcome news waited. Made tea. Watched her. Until Beth could stand it no longer. She called Bridget.

Over the next few days, the grief Beth felt was all-consuming. Bridget stayed by her side all night and into the following day, leaving only after the arrival of Chris.

For the most part, Beth confined herself to her room where she now shared her bed with Dog. She needed him beside her. He would lie with his head between his paws, eyes soulfully watching her as she wept. After six days she was all cried out. Dried up. No more tears would come. What was left was just a great emptiness and sadness the likes of which she'd never before experienced.

After two weeks of being confined to Beth's bedside, Dog was gradually becoming increasingly playful, jumping on and off the bed, dragging off the covers, turning in circles and barking, waiting for Beth to get the message. Telling her it was time for recovery.

Time to stop wallowing. Time to be up and about and making some sort of effort to come to terms with the loss. To stop relying on others. For the whole time, lying grief-stricken in her room, Beth hadn't given a thought to how worrying it must have been for Chris who'd been patiently nurturing, tending and listening. Now she castigated herself for being selfish and she determined to try to make an effort to put her life back together. Chris felt a great sense of relief on the morning that Beth walked downstairs fully dressed, smiled and threw her arms around her sister and wept on her shoulder

'I'm going to be okay, Chris,' she said.

During those weeks there'd been visits from Bridget, Malcolm and James, but Beth had refused to see anyone but Chris. Then came the day when Chris had to tell Beth that she was being put under pressure to return to work. She pleaded with Beth to come back with her to London, but to no avail.

'Chris, you've been an absolute rock,' Beth told her. 'I promise you I'm going to be OK, especially as Bridget insists on mollycoddling me. I have to face up to life without Martin sometime, and the longer I sit around and mope the harder it will be.'

So Chris returned to London and Bridget came and went almost daily, her visits easing off as Beth started getting out and about. During her first couple of brief shopping trips to the village, Beth was subjected to pitying looks and offers of condolences from kindly villagers, and although knowing their concern for her welfare was well-meant, she couldn't bring herself to welcome the attention, preferring instead the anonymity of Durham city. She would often meet Bridget for lunch, Bridget noticing the gradual improvement in Beth's road to recovery. Her smile had returned but the sadness still showed in her eyes. Still, Bridget told herself, it's early days. The important thing was that Beth was coping, which is what she told Chris during one of their bi-weekly telephone conversations.

***

The eventual inquiry into the accident was straightforward. Martin had pulled out from the layby without checking his mirror, right into the path of the juggernaut. There were several reports from other motorists. The driver of a car coming the other way had witnessed the accident and had just managed to swerve in time to avoid being hit himself. And a car travelling at a safe distance behind the juggernaut because of the driving snow had also seen what had happened. All who knew him commented on what an excellent driver Martin was, initially doubting that he could possibly have made such a devastating error of judgment. But the evidence was conclusive. The atrocious weather on the night in question had been the main contributory factor. A verdict of accidental death was recorded. The life assurance company tried to argue the possibility of suicide but this was ruled out, the deceased having shown no signs of depression prior to the night in question. The move to Durham had prompted Beth and Martin to upgrade their life insurances. In the event of either of them dying the house would be paid for and a substantial lump sum provided for the surviving spouse. Beth would have the luxury of not having to work for some time to come, if at all. Nevertheless, she didn't feel any amount of compensation could make up for her loss. Despite their recent difficulties, she missed Martin terribly. And she was convinced that she always would.

***

In the weeks following the small private cremation, when Chris had again been and gone, barely a day went by without a visit from Bridget, James or young Malcolm. Bridget and Malcolm would often arrive together after work, sometimes bringing gifts of food to be shared. They'd also bring treats for Dog who, now having the run of the whole house, was never far from Beth's side and adept at alerting her to the arrival of visitors. 'What would I do without you, Dog?' she'd repeat over and over while running her hand down from his head to his flank. Dog would gaze up at her with an adoring, mournful look, as though sharing the pain. James would also make a point of occasionally calling during the day, knowing that Bridget and Malcolm would be tied up in the office. In the early days, Chris's daily phone calls invariably included a plea for Beth to give serious consideration to packing up and moving back to London. Eventually Chris gave up, instead travelling north every alternate weekend to be with her sister.

Chapter Forty

Sadler would come by every month to collect the rent and Da would be respectful, doffing his cap and callin' him Mr Sadler. And, believe me, Pickie, I could see the same look in Sadler's eyes as I'd seen in Gregory's, and Da's before that. He'd watch me from under those hooded lids when he thought me da wasn't lookin.' He watched how hard I worked and I was afeared when I heard Ma and Da sayin' how awful it was that his two sons had upped and left, leavin' old Sadler to run the place with just his ailin' wife and a couple of part-time hired hands. It was the only time I ever heard me ma sympathise with anyone other than herself. I somehow knew then that one day Sadler'd get his hands on me. It took over five years, Pickie. Five years of toilin' and sweatin' with nowt to show for it except the clothes I stood up in. And it was then the news came of the bereavement. It was said that Sadler's wife died of a broken heart because of bein' abandoned by her boys. But from what I learnt later, I think she died of broken bones and brutal treatment. And I'll bet she was glad her sons had gone away. Glad to have only one bullyin' man to deal with instead of three. The gossip I overheard between Da and Ma was that folks said those sons were a cruel pair from the start and that the village would be a better place without them. 'Evil will out,' was what people said. I was twenty-two when Da made the deal with Sadler. And, believe me Pickie, I'd sooner have stayed where I was.

Forty-One

Beth had taken to spending more time in the studio, often simply sitting gazing out at the view through the huge windows, thinking more and more about young Bessie Ellis and neglecting any attempt at jewellery-making. Instead, her work table was covered in beautiful vibrant silk threads and a variety of pieces of coloured silk fabric. Together, James and Malcolm had brought one of the armchairs from the lounge down into the studio so she could sit in comfort listening to music while she sewed. Somehow, the pleasure she got from creating beautiful pieces of embroidery had the effect of helping to ease the horrors of the past weeks, providing longed-for respite for the hours she spent alone with Dog. Having initially worked on linen, Beth became more confident and now that she was working on silk, the results were proving to be even more beautiful.

It had come as a surprise to her, the enjoyment she got from sewing. She had purchased a number of books on the subject, as well as on the history of embroidery and a practical instruction book of complicated stitches, referring to them when there was a design in her head that she was unsure of how to achieve. More and more often, when deliberating on how to proceed on a particular piece, she would find herself fingering the black and white pendant which she now wore constantly. Each time, her thoughts would turn to the sad story of the young laundry maid who had been badly used by Gregory, the man who Beth was now convinced was Martin's dissolute ancestor. Martin would never know how she had spent time researching his ancestry.

***

With the death of Martin, a temporary replacement was sent up from London to help out with the crisis in the office. He was a sharp-suited thirty-something man called Brian Jessop. It seemed to Harold, who had been hoping to take over the running of the agency now that both Martin and Fiona were gone, that his hopes might be dashed. But his initial resentment of the presence of Jessop was somewhat alleviated when Jessop assured him he was simply there to assist with the recruitment, the most urgent issue being to find a replacement for Martin. The Durham branch had been doing so well under his management that head office wanted to ensure it continued to flourish, and it wouldn't be possible for it to continue growing without a competent senior negotiator at the helm.

Immediately, Harold set out to prove he had what it took to step into Martin's shoes. The first week of foregoing his nightly pub visits was a challenge but the benefits of being on the wagon were beginning to show.

He started arriving at the office early and leaving late, applying himself diligently to the workload until even Bridget and Malcolm had to accede grudging admiration for his efforts. He was going all out to make an impression upon Jessop and he felt he was succeeding.

Replacement, my arse, Harold told himself. *This is my chance and I don't intend to fuck it up*.

There was only one drawback to his determination, which was his growing obsession with Beth. Several times during the day he'd find her intruding on his thoughts, picturing her petite stature, pretty face and glossy, unruly hair. He just couldn't get her out of his mind, even though she no longer popped into the office. There was no reason for her to do so. He remembered the shock on her face the night of the party when everything had gone tits up, and the noticeable devastation wrought by the death of Martin. He'd been pleased to have been out of it on the night Fiona's broken body was discovered. He wouldn't have wanted to see that. And now the lovely Beth was a widow. A young, beautiful widow. Grieving. He wanted to comfort her. Well, he wanted to do more than that. He wanted her, full stop. He'd wanted her from the first time he saw her. It had been several weeks since the funeral and he'd managed to keep his distance so far, but with the thought of her eating away at him night and day, he knew it wouldn't be long before he'd need to do something about it. *What the hell! She's lonely. She's*

isolated. And she's in need of some tender loving care.
He decided now might be the opportune time to make
his move.

Chapter Forty-Two

William had just turned five when Sadler came for me. William was a monster. Treated me the same as Ma and Da did. How else would he be, seein' as how they treated me and him learnin' from it? I don't even know if he was ever told I was his sister. Ma and Da just called me her or she or it. As far as the boy could tell, I was of no more consequence than one of the farm animals. He had the same eyes as me da, did William. And the same bullyin' way with him. He would lash out at me when I was passin' and wouldn't be chastised. Da laughed when William, young though he was, would kick me bad leg and call me a useless cripple. He learnt it from Da. I slapped him once, thinkin' nobody could see. I didn't do it again after the beatin' I got. But I couldn't help meself, Pickie. Me life had been made worse with the comin' of William. But, even so, that didn't mean I wanted to be sent to Sadler. I thought I was mebbe too useful to Da and Ma for them to let me go. It was only when I saw the purse bein' put into Da's greedy graspin' hands that I knew I'd have no choice. If I could've run, I would've done. But how far would I have got with me useless leg? I was forced to go with him there and then. It was just sprung on me. Out of the blue. And it wasn't as though I had to gather me things. What did I have? Only the clothes I stood up in and little else. The only thing I had of value was the plain little sewin' bag that Mrs Bull had given me as a partin' gift. I treasured that bag and its contents. Needles, pins, a little thimble and pretty threads and buttons. For nearly five years I'd managed to keep it hidden. When I pulled it out that day it was covered in cobwebs and dust. But I was relieved that the mice hadn't got to it. I quickly pulled up me skirt and stuffed it in the top of me drawers under me petticoat, hopin' I wouldn't be stabbed by a stray needle. Ma and Da didn't wave to me as I stepped up onto Sadler's cart and was took. They just stood on the doorstep and watched. Didn't so much as say goodbye, Pickie. Just watched the cart pull away. Mebbe Sadler had paid enough for them to employ another poor skivvy. I feel sorry for her if they did. However much it was, it must've been enough for them to be glad to see the back of me. Mebbe I'd always been too much of an embarrassment. I wondered then, as I sat in that cart, if I was destined to be bought and sold forever. I wasn't a daughter as far as they were concerned. I was a chattel.

Chapter Forty-Three

Having volunteered to lock up the office after close of business that day, citing the mounting paperwork he needed to get through, Harold waited until everybody had left, intending to make his first call on Beth since the tragedy. He armed himself with a bunch of second-rate flowers from the garage and drove to Lanchester, fortifying himself on the way with his first drink in over two weeks. Turning onto the track leading up to the house, he suddenly braked. No, he wasn't mistaken. He recognised the two cars in the driveway. 'Shit!' he cursed. 'Bloody Bridget and Malcolm.' What were they doing here? Had they been calling in on Beth all this time without telling him, or was this a one-off. A sudden joint decision as they'd left the office? He backed up, disappointed. He'd have to leave it for another day.

The next morning, he kept stealing surreptitious glances at the pair. He wanted to find out if their visits were a regular thing but could hardly ask without revealing that he'd been about to visit Beth himself. They might suspect his motives. But he was peeved that they hadn't thought fit to include him in their visit.

'I wonder how poor Beth's doing,' he said to Bridget.

'I've visited her now and then,' replied Bridget. 'As you'd expect, Martin's death has taken its toll. It's going to take quite a while before she gets over it.' Bridget thought it was nice of Harold to be concerned. The subject of the loss of Martin hadn't been mentioned much around the office after the initial few days. There had been very little surmising about how Martin could have been so careless as to pull out in front of fast-moving traffic without checking. It had seemed too voyeuristic to gossip about the whys and wherefores of the tragedy, especially, Bridget suspected, as the question of suicide, although not mentioned, was lurking somewhere in the back of people's minds. Bridget herself didn't believe for one minute that that was the case.

***

Harold decided not to risk another evening visit in case Malcolm and/or Bridget turned up. He took the afternoon off, selected what he considered an attractive bunch of mixed blooms from M&S and made his way to Lanchester. On the way there he reckoned that a bit of Dutch courage was called for. He was nervous. How would Beth react? He hadn't had any contact with her since the funeral. He sat with his pint, mulling it over. He'd tell her he hadn't called because he thought she'd needed the space to come to terms with her loss, but hoped his visit would go some way to letting her know that she was in his thoughts. That he'd always thought highly of her. Shit! Maybe that wasn't the way to go about it. He went to the bar and ordered a second pint with a whisky chaser. He'd have to make that the last otherwise he'd be well over the limit. But the trouble was, having been off the booze for a few weeks, he was quickly back in the swing of things. With each sip his confidence grew until he convinced himself that, from the start, he'd sensed a connection between himself and Beth. Looking back, he was sure they'd exchanged that spark of electricity. That didn't happen unless the feeling was mutual. He'd risk one more round. How many had he had? He wasn't sure. Still, he was halfway to Lanchester anyway so the rest of the drive would take less than ten minutes. It was almost four o'clock when he finally decided he'd better get going, confident now that he'd receive a warm welcome. Or, hopefully, a *very* warm welcome. A young and beautiful widow has needs. But he knew he had to tread carefully. Give no indication of his feelings on the first visit. Take it slowly. Invite her out to dinner. No strings attached. He didn't want to frighten her off. He pulled himself away from the bar and made his way to the toilet. Can't turn up with a full bloody bladder, he thought. That would put the mockers on it. Having to run to the bloody toilet almost before he got to say hello.

Chapter Forty-Four

Her sadness hurts me, Pickie. But I'm not sorry. He had to be got rid of. Him as what was no good for her. Better hurtin' now than later. If we hadn't got rid of him mebbe she'd have had a bairn with him. I couldn't allow that. Not with him.

Look what me bonnie's doin', Pickie. See how expertly she uses the needle. Look at the puttin' together of the colours. She's creatin' really beautiful pieces. No old bits of rag for me bonnie to work on. She's workin' on silk. I know it's silk because of me handlin' of Henrietta's fine gowns. I used to fondle them as I mended them. Did I dream of ownin' such beautiful clothes? I suppose I did. Even though I knew it could never happen. The likes of me would never get to wear anythin' other than plain cotton or wool, mended time and time again until they became rags. It makes me proud that me bonnie's so clever. And it tears me heartstrings to feel her grief. But it had to be done. Our yew needed the nourishment we're providin'. She uses us and we use her. That's just the way it is.

It would be good to think that me bonnie knows we're looking after her. But if she knew, mebbe she'd think we're evil. That what we did robbed her of happiness. I couldn't bear that, Pickie. We're protectin' her. Gettin' rid of those who harmed me and you and them what would harm me bonnie. Teachin' lessons. An eye for an eye, no matter how long it takes. Somebody has to suffer for the sufferin' I was put through. Now that we've started, I'm gettin' a taste for it Pickie. After the next one, I'm not sure I'll be able to stop. Mebbe our yew will put us to rest again for a while. Work her magic and put us to slumberin'. Or mebbe she won't. If she wants more then she'll have more. She's been kind to us and we're glad to do her biddin'. It's just a pity that we had to wait. I suppose if I did then what we're doin' now, I'd likely have ended up on the gallows. Or mebbe, because of me club foot they'd think me brain was addled. Then I might've been put in an asylum, livin' out me life in the company of lunatics. Would that've been better than what happened to me? I don't think so because then I wouldn't have you beside me, Pickie.

Chapter Forty-Five

Beth hadn't heard the car drive up but was alerted by a growl from Dog before the doorbell rang. And she was surprised, and not a little put out, when she opened the door and found Harold standing there clutching flowers and a bottle. He was the last person she either expected or wanted to see. She could smell the drink on him and was reluctant to let him in.

'I'm sorry I haven't called before, Beth,' he said, looking sheepish, 'but I didn't want to intrude on your grief. I happened to finish early and thought I'd drop by to pay my respects seeing as how I didn't get to talk to you much at Martin's funeral. Just wondered how you're doing and thinking you might appreciate a bit of company.'

Beth was in two minds. On the one hand she didn't want to appear rude or ungrateful, but on the other, she didn't relish spending any time with her unwelcome visitor.

'Would it be all right to come in for a minute?' he asked.

Beth still hadn't said anything. His visit was so unexpected that she was momentarily in a state of flux.

She hoped she didn't look as unwelcoming as she was feeling. She pulled herself together.

'I'm sorry, Harold,' she said. 'You must think me very rude. Of course you can come in.' She stepped aside as he entered, hoping she could come up with a reason to ensure the visit would be as brief as possible. She'd never before been alone with Harold and she didn't entirely trust him. She was remembering the night of the housewarming and how his eyes had seemed to follow her wherever she moved. Taking comfort from the presence of Dog who, although slouching in an almost predatory manner, nevertheless hadn't growled at her visitor, she led the way upstairs.

Standing in the lounge, Harold handed over the bunch of flowers and a bottle of wine he'd stopped and bought on the way.

'So, how have you been managing, Beth? I'm really sorry for the way things have turned out for you. I can't imagine how you're feeling.'

Beth thought he looked genuine. She told him to take a seat and thanked him for the gifts. She supposed she should offer him a glass of something even though she didn't want to drink anything herself.

'It's kind of you to think of me, Harold. I'm not doing so badly considering. Can I offer you a glass of wine?'

To her surprise, Harold declined, opting instead for coffee. 'Bit of a drive to get home,' he said, 'and this bloody weather doesn't help.' He suddenly seemed to realise what he'd said. The last thing he wanted was to remind Beth of Martin's accident. He was relieved to see that she didn't react. She just turned and went into the kitchen to make him a coffee. *Me and my big mouth*, he thought to himself, looking around and admiring the room with its soft lighting and tasteful furnishings. He was thinking how living in a place like this would solve all his problems. He just couldn't go on much longer having to share a grotty house with cretins. He'd have to take it slowly though. Win her over. He'd made a mistake by stopping off at the pub but he didn't think she'd smelt the booze on him. At least she hadn't given any indication that she had.

Beth returned and handed him his coffee, hoping he'd drink it quickly and be gone.

'Lovely place you have here, Beth,' he said. 'You must be really proud of what you've achieved.'

Beth simply nodded and smiled then asked him how things were going at the agency, making small talk. Harold told her how much they all missed Martin and that the guy who had been sent from London, who he remembered had been at Martin's funeral, was happy with the way things were going. His visit had been fleeting and he'd been satisfied to leave the initial interviews in Harold's hands. Once a shortlist had been produced, he'd be back to conduct second interviews.

Beth was happy to let Harold talk and tried to show some interest in what he was saying but, in truth, she couldn't care less about the business and had little to say. Besides, she already knew what was going on, having been updated on a regular basis by Bridget and Malcolm. She was relieved when Harold finished his coffee and said he must be getting along. She accompanied him to the door, taking pains to keep her distance. She still didn't trust him and was thankful that he didn't make any move to hug her or give her a peck on the cheek as he left. In fact, she thought, despite her reservations, Harold had acted like the perfect gentleman. As had Dog.

Chapter Forty-Six

What did I tell you, Pickie? Sneaky. Just the same. As I've heard others say, 'the apple doesn't fall far from the tree.' Bidin' his time. Tryin' to fool her into thinkin' she can trust him. He fooled me all right in the beginnin'. I thought I knew what would be in store for me as soon as he got me on me own. But it didn't happen. Not at first. He led me on. Pretendin' he wasn't interested. Lettin' me settle. Lullin' me into thinkin' I was in a safe place. That's just what he's doin' now with me bonnie. Lullin' her. Hidin' his intentions. Like I said. Sneaky.

Chapter Forty-Seven

Chris' weekend visits invariably included a get - together with James who they'd either somehow *accidentally* bump into when shopping, or who would turn up unexpectedly on the doorstep. Chris insisted it was just coincidence, but Beth suspected not. She hadn't failed to notice the shared looks and the fact that Chris had toned down her usual flamboyant style, opting instead for a more sophisticated but not quite sedate look. Beth wondered if Chris's denial of any burgeoning romance was because she was reluctant to flaunt any hint of happiness when Beth herself was still mourning the loss of Martin.

To counter this, Beth would suddenly pull out of planned lunch or dinner dates with James and Chris, citing a variety of excuses, and insisting they go without her. Bridget and Malcolm, knowing that Beth had her sister staying at the weekends, mainly confined their visits to weekdays when they knew Beth would be devoid of much-needed company.

The truth was that Beth enjoyed being alone with Dog. She was able to lose herself in working on the intricate construction of her latest embroidery project with no interruptions. Nobody fussing over her, however well-intentioned. She found that early afternoons on weekdays were the optimum times to concentrate, knowing that Bridget and Malcolm would be at work.

It had been almost a week since the visit from Harold, but he'd taken to calling her every other day, ostensibly to ask how she was bearing up and to ask if there was anything he could do. Each time he got the same answer. She was fine and no, there was nothing she needed. She'd confided in Bridget and Chris, telling them about his afternoon visit which had come out of the blue, but she assured them that he hadn't behaved inappropriately and they therefore had nothing to worry about. Nevertheless, Chris had asked Bridget to keep an eye on the situation. The last thing Beth needed at the moment was to be bombarded with unwelcome attention.

***

Harold was having doubts about being up to the management job. He was out and about more and more often, both during the day and in the evenings, carrying out valuations, doing his best to make sure business didn't slacken off too much following Martin's untimely demise. And, when in the office, he was having to continue conducting interviews for potential replacement staff in order to produce a shortlist for head office, which they were expecting before the end of the month. He was playing it canny, being careful to exclude the CVs of those candidates he considered too suitable, hoping to get the message across that he himself was the best man for the job. But the paperwork was overwhelming. He had to grudgingly admit that he wouldn't be able to keep up if it wasn't for Bridget who, it had to be said, relieved him of more than her fair share. He found himself having to rely on Malcolm to conduct some of the less desirable property valuations, even though he wasn't yet fully qualified. Nevertheless, the lad had risen to the challenge and seemed to know what he was doing. The branch had built up quite a reputation during those early days when Martin was in charge. As a consequence, the enquiries continued to flood in. The sooner they got some help the better, but preferably from someone not overly ambitious. Definitely not someone with proven management and sales experience.

Christ, it was all so tiring. He didn't think he could cope with the pace for too much longer. Exhaustion was setting in. What he needed was a bloody good piss-up to take his mind off it all. And a good fuck wouldn't go amiss. But not any old fuck. He was done with that. He was set on the ultimate prize. He'd have to make another move soon. Continue to take it slowly, though. Didn't want to frighten her off.

As far as Bridget was concerned, the few interviewees Harold had recommended to head office were woefully inadequate. He appeared to have overestimated their capabilities. She knew it wasn't her place to interfere, Harold being temporarily in charge, and she could hardly admit that she'd been through all the applications without his knowledge. It appeared he was discounting the most experienced in favour of those less knowledgeable and without proven track records. She felt she knew what game he was playing. He was after the management job himself. She was in no doubt that Harold just didn't have the managerial skills necessary to run the place the way Martin had. She could envision the decline in sales if Harold got his way, the eventual closure of the branch if it became unviable and herself out on her ear. She had nothing against Harold apart from his lackadaisical attitude and beer breath, that is, although, if she was truthful, he did seem to be making more of an effort lately. She mentioned it to Beth.

'Have you any advice?' she asked.

'To be honest, Bridget, the success or otherwise of the agency isn't anything I've given thought to. But I can understand why you're worried.'

'It's not only my own situation that worries me, I'd hate to see young Malcolm being thrust out of a job when he's worked so hard.'

'Well, it seems to me that you can only hope. If he does manage to convince them that he's the best man for the job then fails to deliver, head office will reach their own decision and there's not much you can do about it. Sadly, they're not likely to ask your opinion on the viability of Harold as manager, despite your vast experience. Female administrators and secretaries are rarely consulted on these things. We women still have a way to go in the workplace, I'm afraid.

'Speaking of Harold, have you had a repeat visit?' Bridget asked.

'No, thank God, although I honestly don't think he had any ulterior motives. I think my original assessment of him was skewed just because he paid me a little too much attention. It may be that he thought complimenting the boss's wife would stand him in good stead. With Martin gone, there's no point. I think the wine and flowers were simply out of genuine concern and I think I'm guilty of an error of judgment when it comes to Harold and his motives. I don't particularly like him, but I think he's harmless. He occasionally rings to ask how I am and has once or twice asked me if I fancy having a night out somewhere, but I'm sure he'll soon tire of that, and it's unlikely I'll get another visit.'

Bridget wasn't so convinced.

Chapter Forty-Eight

Bert Sadler wasn't so bad those first few weeks. As long as I cleaned and cooked to his likin' he let me be. If I'm honest, I'd begun to believe that I was better off there than I ever was at home. Not that it was ever a home. It was like I'd been let out of prison. Bert didn't talk to me much. Only to tell me what sort of food he liked and what he wanted doin'. Which was a lot less than me own ma and da had made me do. But I should have known better, Pickie. I'd seen the way he'd looked at me over the years. He was only bidin' his time to put me off me guard. Before long he got down to the real reason for buyin' me. He'd been quaffin' back ale durin' supper and I could see him eyein' me as I went about me chores. There was no bolt on me bedroom door, not that that would have stopped him, brute that he was. He was rough that first night and when he went to his own room I wept for the cruelty of it, more's the pity. I should have got angry. Not lay there wallowin' in self-pity. But our yew hadn't got me then so I hadn't lost me meekness. That's what I was then, Pickie. Cowerin' and meek. And for all me pain, nobody paid for their wrongdoin'. For turnin' me into what I've become. Until now. Our yew has put the vengeance in me. She's shown me the power of retribution. It's what she needs, and it's what I crave. Why should I have been put to rot. Forgotten. As though I'd never been. She's put the fury in me and I'm grateful. She's the only true mother I've ever known. The only thing to truly embrace me and give me comfort.

If I'd known what was to come mebbe I'd've fought back that first time. Bashed him with somethin'. Killed him mebbe.

You were a real comfort to me during that time, Pickie. I couldn't abide leavin' you outside, shiverin' during those bleak winter days. But there was nowt I could do durin' the nights when he was home. That first time he caught you in the kitchen he gave you a kickin'. You remember, Pickie? But when he was out, I'd make sure you came inside to the warm and I'd give you food. I couldn't believe how skinny you were when I first saw you. Skinny and cowerin'. Tethered to that shack that was barely big enough for you to turn round in. And your ribs were showin'. I couldn't see what use he had of you, other than to kick. You were me only friend. Until Tinker came along.

Chapter Forty-Nine

Despite the ongoing numerous pleas by Chris, Beth still adamantly refused to spend Christmas in London.

'I just couldn't leave Dog,' she insisted. 'And please don't suggest that I put him in kennels. It would feel like a betrayal of trust.'

'Don't you think it would be good for you to get away for a while after all that's happened? I worry about you, Beth.'

'I really wish you wouldn't, Chris,' Beth countered.

'Then that's settled. If I can't persuade you to come down to the bright lights I'm coming up to spend Christmas with you. There's no way I'm allowing you to wallow in grief over the festive season. And we're going to be out and about. Shopping, and wining and dining non-stop, okay? We're going to have some fun, Beth. Fun! Remember what that is? Mind you, shopping will, of necessity, be our first priority. We need to seek out suitable gear to cope with the arctic conditions. You know I can't bear the bloody cold.'

Ending the call, Chris rang Bridget to ask her to find a suitable venue for a get-together either in the few days before Christmas or shortly after, giving her the dates of her arrival and departure from Durham. Bridget said that she'd get on the case immediately before everything was booked solid.

'How many for?' asked Bridget.

'Well, I'm thinking you, me and Beth, of course, plus I'll check with James and get back to you. Oh, and why don't we invite young Malcolm as well? Going on first impressions, he seems to be a good person to have around with his cheerful demeanour and handsome, smiling face.'

'Not Harold?'

'I don't think so Bridget, do you? After the way he behaved at the housewarming I think we can do without his company. I'm no saint myself when it comes to overindulgence but, as far as I'm aware, I've never passed out at the dinner table. Maybe afterwards.' Chris laughed. 'And I have been accused of a tendency to sing loudly and badly when under the influence. Never could hold a tune. Anyway, back to the point, I can't say I like the man much and I'd rather not have him anywhere near Beth. I don't entirely trust him and she's still pretty vulnerable.'

'I take your point, Chris, and if it's any consolation, I feel exactly the same way,' agreed Bridget.

Chapter Fifty

Tinker was nice, Pickie. He had a happy face. Remember? Always smilin'. Even though life was hard for him, travellin' round the country doing the sharpenin' for just a few pennies. I always made sure there was a couple of knives and some scissors for him to work on. And when he'd done, he'd have a pot of strong tea and spend a few minutes chattin'. We looked forward to him comin', didn't we, Pickie? But we had to keep a lookout in case Bert came home and found me dishin' out hospitality to the likes of Tinker. That one time he'd found me passin' Tinker a pot of tea, he knocked it out of me hand and told Tinker to bugger off before he kicked his arse, turnin' to me and sayin', 'I won't be havin' you cavortin' with no filthy tinker boy.' Cavortin'! That's what he called it. Poor Tinker. He scarpered as though the hounds of hell were after him. We had to be careful after that, didn't we? The knives still needed sharpenin', and Tinker still came back even though Bert had put the fear of God into him, Bert bein' so much bigger and stronger than Tinker. I think Tinker felt sorry for me, whether because of me foot or because of havin' to live with Bert, I'll never know. And, I remember, there was nowt but friendship in that happy, open face. I would've recognised the other. If there'd been even a hint of lust, I'd have seen it, Pickie. Tinker was just nice.

Chapter Fifty-One

Arriving at the office the following morning, Harold entered just as Bridget was saying, 'A table for five at seven thirty on the twenty-second?' There was a short pause before she added, 'You have? That's marvellous. I was beginning to give up. Everywhere else I've tried has been fully booked. Thank you. We'll see you then.' She put the phone down.

'Planning a pre-Christmas celebration, Bridget?' commented Harold. 'Family?'

'Just a few friends,' answered Bridget, unable to hide the guilty blush that she felt was evident. She turned away quickly to concentrate on the pile of files waiting to be updated.

Chapter Fifty-Two

It seemed the more Bert used me the nastier he became. After that first time he'd get angry with me for no reason. I did everythin' he told me to and more, hopin' to please him for fear of his tongue. He didn't hit me in those first few weeks. That only started the day he came home and found me sitting on the old cracket by the fire stitchin'. When he saw what I was doin' he snatched it from me. It was a wee hankie I was embroiderin' and hopin' to send as a gift to Mrs Bull for bein' kind to me. I missed Mrs Bull. I'd already hemmed the edges of the little scrap of linen I'd cut from a worn old sheet and I was concentration' so hard that I didn't hear him comin' in. Bert scrunched it up in his big fist and threw it on the fire. 'I'll not have you wastin' your time on fancy work when there's plenty of proper work to be gettin' on with,' he said. That was the first time he lashed out, and the clout knocked me off me stool. He should've had the sense to take me needlework bag as well because that clout only made me determined to start makin' another one. Bert Sadler was a big, stupid bully and even after so many beatin's at the hands of me da, there was still a bit of a spark in me, Pickie. I wasn't entirely beaten. Not then.

Chapter Fifty-Three

After work, Bridget and Malcolm went together to call on Beth. Malcolm looked forward to their visits, always finding something new to admire in the way the house was constructed and to marvel at how Beth had turned it into such a beautiful home. They arrived to find Beth sorting through boxes in the garage, a couple of boxes half emptied, piles of books already stacked on the floor and Beth sweating with the effort.

'Still unpacking after all this time?' asked Bridget.

Beth wiped her brow with her sleeve. 'There's a lot more than I remember and it's proving to be a much bigger task than I anticipated. Apart from the books, there's a box full of pictures that should have been hung on the walls by now.'

'Can we help?' asked Malcolm.

'Absolutely not,' Beth replied. 'I'm really pleased to see you both and I'm not spending our time together carting things up the stairs when we can be sitting chatting. Anyway, the physical activity has made me thirsty so I think I could do with a glass of wine. You'll join me, won't you Bridget?'

'I think it would be rude not to,' said Bridget, and they made their way upstairs.

Malcolm and Dog had taken a great liking to each other. Malcolm would sit petting him while the three of them chatted over coffee, or, in Bridget and Beth's case, a glass or two of wine. He admired Beth's apparent determination to try to put the recent tragedies behind her, noting that during the last few visits it seemed to him that she had begun to smile more.

'Do you think we're being unfair not asking Harold to this dinner?' Beth asked, looking at each of them in turn.

'No, I don't,' answered Bridget, adamant. 'I don't think any of us particularly enjoy his company. What do you think, Malcolm?'

Malcolm wasn't sure his opinion mattered but he answered anyway. 'I feel a bit guilty but, then again, after the way he behaved at the housewarming, I don't particularly fancy sitting through what should be a nice get-together with a drunken Harold.'

'I'm thinking life could be made difficult for you both if Harold ever found out that we'd deliberately excluded him,' Beth said. 'And, after all, it's a Christmas celebration. Peace to all men etcetera.'

Bridget considered this then said, 'It might be a good idea to check with Chris and James. I know Chris definitely didn't want to include him. Obviously, I don't know what James thinks but he'll probably go along with whatever Chris says.'

There was silence for a few minutes as they each considered the implications of the decision to include Harold or not.

'Changing the subject,' said Beth, watching Dog resting his head on Malcolm's lap while Malcolm continued to fondle him, 'Dog really seems to like you Malcolm. It's not often he leaves my side to sit beside somebody else. He's particular about who he likes, who he seems to dislike, and who he's indifferent to. Pretty pickie, when all's said and done.'

At this, Dog's ears pricked up and he wandered over to Beth, plonking himself down beside her. She scratched him behind his ear, ruffled his head and said, 'You're pickie, aren't you Dog. After all this time of calling you simply Dog, I think from now on you should be known as Pickie,' she joked.

'I don't think he'll go for it, Beth, said Bridget, laughing. 'By now he must be so used to you calling him Dog, that a change of name won't work.'

But Beth thought the name suited Dog, and hadn't she always meant to give him a proper name? It was just that until now she hadn't been able to find a name that seemed to fit. She wondered if it was too late. Nevertheless, she was intrigued, as was Malcolm. 'Why don't you put it to the test Beth? He suggested, giving that boyish grin that Beth found so endearing.

'I'll see,' she said.

On the way out, the inner door to the garage remaining open, Malcolm couldn't help but notice the number of unopened boxes Beth had yet to deal with. He didn't want to seem forward but he really felt the urge to help. He steeled himself and, blushing, he said, 'Beth, that's quite a task you have getting all that stuff up the stairs. Why don't you leave it and I'll come over one evening, and help?'

'That's so kind of you,' Beth replied, 'but I'm sure I can manage. Mind you, on second thoughts, what I know for certain I can't manage though is hanging the pictures, some of which are pretty heavy. Are you any good at that, Malcolm? Your help in that respect would be very much appreciated.'

'No problem.' Malcolm was chuffed that his offer to help was welcome. 'I'll be really glad to help. My dad's great at DIY and he made sure he taught me everything he knows in that respect. He's not the sort of man to spend money on professional help when he can do a job himself. I'll borrow his drill and bring anything else I might need. When would you like me to come?'

'Well, I was hoping to get them hung before Christmas, but it's entirely up to you and your availability.'

'Sometime next week? Tuesday after work?'

'I'll come along as well,' chirped up Bridget, 'to lend an extra hand.'

'That would be wonderful. Thank you both so much. And, I tell you what, how about I cook the three of us a really nice meal for when the job's done.'

As they stood on the doorstep saying their goodbyes, Dog having disappeared on his usual jaunt behind the house to circle around the old yew tree, Malcolm said, 'Go on, Beth. Give it a try before we go. Call for Dog by his new name.'

Beth and Bridget laughed as Bridget said, 'I doubt it will work, but satisfy the lad's curiosity and give it a go, Beth, before we all freeze to death out here.'

'Pickie,' Beth called out, and a minute later Dog was by her side.'

'Well, I never,' commented Bridget. 'Surely must be a fluke. Must have been on his way back to you anyway.'

Beth wondered. She'd try calling Dog Pickie for the next couple of days and see if he responded. Malcolm and Bridget took their leave and Beth thought it had been one of the most pleasant evenings she'd had since the fateful evening of Martin's accident.

Chapter Fifty-Four

*It took me a long time to make that hankie, Pickie,
workin' by candle in me room when Bert was passed out
with the drink. Until I saw me babbie clutchin' it, I
hadn't known whether Tinker'd managed to get it to
Mrs Bull. Now that I know he did, it gladdens me heart,
black though it's become. I'd finished the hankie to me
satisfaction and I knew there was only one way to get it
to Mrs Bull. I was so proud of it, Pickie. I showed it to
Tinker. He said it was the most beautiful thing he'd ever
seen. When I told him who it was for, he told me that he
had to go to Hill House every month to do the
sharpenin', but the cutlery and utensils were brought
out to him to carry out his work in the yard. He didn't
know Mrs Bull, and he didn't know where to look to find
her. I'd told Tinker how kind she was to me when he was
lingerin' over his mug of tea, always on the lookout for
Bert. If Bert did happen to show up, Tinker always
managed to somehow hide his mug on the little shelf
behind his grindin' wheel. He didn't want me to get in
trouble with Bert, seein' as how he'd behaved that first
time. Tinker promised to get the hankie to Mrs Bull and
he'd make sure to tell her it was from me for all her
kindness. I would've liked to have written a note to go*

*with it but I'd never had the learnin'. I told him he
needed to go to the big double black doors to the left of
the servant's entrance round the back. That was where
the laundry was. He wasn't to hand it to anybody but
Mrs Bull. I wanted to make sure she got it and not some
thievin' scullery maid.*

Chapter Fifty-Five

Harold's few invitations over the phone for Beth to join him for a quiet drink or a meal out had been rejected, even though he'd thought he'd been the perfect gentleman. Perhaps it was time for another visit. He needed her to see that he only had her best interests at heart; let her know that he worried about her being alone on the run-up to Christmas when the loss of Martin would weigh heavily. *Yes*, he thought, *that's the best approach*. And after all, it was true. Besotted he might be, but he didn't want to rush things. With women like Beth, the softly, softly approach was needed.

***

Chris arrived as usual, mid-morning on Saturday, and they spent the day hunting out gifts for Bridget, Malcolm and James, which they planned to take along to the restaurant when they went for their pre-Christmas celebration. By late afternoon they were laden down with bags of heavyweight sweaters, padded coats, hats and boots for themselves, plus the presents, resulting in them both feeling absolutely exhausted. Chris suggested that, rather than bother to cook at home, and as it was so late in the day, they find a half-decent restaurant. 'Anyway,' she added, 'I don't know about you but I'm desperate for a glass of something warming.' Having dumped their purchases in the car, they made their way back to The Market Tavern.

'Are we likely to *accidentally* bump into James, do you think?' asked Beth knowingly when Chris had returned from the bar with their drinks.

'I'd say it was highly likely being as I've just texted him our location,' smiled Chris.

Beth reached across the table and grabbed her sister's hand. 'You're quite smitten, aren't you?' she said, looking lovingly into Chris's eyes. 'I'm truly happy for you both, Chris. James is a lovely man, and he seems equally smitten.'

'I really like him, Beth. I just hope I don't fuck it up this time. I don't have a great history when it comes to matters of the heart. I think men tend to find me a bit challenging, what with my loud mouth and uncompromising attitude.'

It was the first time Beth had seen Chris looking vulnerable and unsure of herself. 'Well, it hasn't put James off so far. From what I've seen he seems to like you just the way you are.'

As she was saying this, the door to the bar opened.

'Oh, shit,' hissed Chris and, before she could say anything else, Harold was hovering at their table.

'Well, well, this is a pleasant surprise,' he said, eyes on Beth. 'Fancy running into you two ladies. Mind if I join you?' He sat himself down beside Beth. 'Now then, I'm sure you'll both join me in a drink, so what are you having?' He hadn't seen Chris since the funeral and noted that she wasn't looking too happy.

'Actually, Harold, we only popped in for one so I'm afraid we can't stay,' Chris said.

'Ah, just one for the road! It's not often I get to sit with two such lovely ladies.' He turned to Beth. 'You'll have another won't you, Beth?'

Beth hesitated, then said, 'I'm driving, Harold, but, if you insist, then I'll have a lemonade.' She thought it would be rude to refuse.

'And I'll have a large Jamieson's,' said Chris. 'Neat, no ice.'

'Grand,' smiled Harold as he got up and made his way to the bar, thinking as he went that Beth's sister was a monumental pain in the arse.

Chris immediately pulled out her phone and texted James.

Change of plan. Fancy a take-away at Beth's?

The reply came almost at once.

What time?

7 o'clock?

Will be there X

Harold returned with the drinks, brushing his hand across Beth's shoulders as he sat down and then adjusting his chair so it was a little closer to her. 'Lovely to see you, Beth,' he said, looking directly into her eyes. She blushed and turned away.

Chris took a large swig of her whisky and said, 'And me?' determined to dominate the conversation, recognising Beth's discomfort.

There was a slight hesitation before Harold answered 'Of course. How are things down in the smoke.'

'Oh, you know. Smoking. Is this one of your regular haunts?'

Harold sensed the animosity. 'One of a few, mainly at the weekend.'

'That's good to know,' Chris said, stopping herself from adding, *a place to avoid in the future then.*

Beth could see the signs. She knew her sister and if they didn't get out of here quickly, this wouldn't end well, especially as Chris was now on the whisky. She made a point of looking at her watch. 'Oh dear. Sorry Harold. I'm afraid we have to run. Time's just about up on the parking meter.'

'Ah, now that's a shame and a great disappointment. Can't you just go and top it up and stay for a little while longer?'

'No can do,' piped up Chris. 'Things to do. People to see. C'mon, sis. Thanks for the drink, Harold.'

'Yes, thank you,' added Beth. 'If I don't see you before, I hope you have a good Christmas,' she added.

'Maybe we can get together before then, Beth. What do you say?'

Beth floundered, finally managing to simply say, 'We'll see.'

'I don't know how you're going to find the time Beth, what, with all those orders to get out over the next couple of weeks,' said Chris, pointedly. 'You're working flat out, aren't you?' She turned to Harold. 'Now, we really do need to get going.'

They gathered their things and quickly left, leaving Harold in no doubt that Beth's sister was a bitch of the highest order who could put a spanner in the works.

As soon as they were outside, Chris said, 'What a fucking creep.'

'He's not that bad Chris. Mebbe he's just a bit lonely.'

'Did you just say "mebbe"?'

'Did I? Must be subconsciously adopting the local dialect.'

James arrived spot on time and the three of them enjoyed a happy evening dining on Indian take-away washed down with copious amounts of wine. By ten o'clock, Beth was too tired to stay up any longer so she said goodnight and took herself off to bed, Pickie following at her heels.

Rising early on Sunday morning, she wasn't overly surprised to see James's jacket over the arm of the couch. She smiled to herself and hoped that her sister had finally found the man she wanted to settle down with.

***

Harold spent the rest of the weekend thinking about Beth. She'd looked so beautiful and fragile when he'd seen her in the pub and he couldn't get her out of his mind. It was like he was obsessed. Never before had he wanted a woman so badly, and he'd had plenty over the years. It was almost as though she'd put a spell on him. He laughed at this notion, telling himself he was being ridiculous. He was just a horny bastard. But, given the chance, he truly believed he would gladly give up playing the field forever if he could have Beth. He sat on the bar stool of his local and put his head in his hands, thinking, *Jesus, how the hell can I concentrate on anything when all I can think of is that bloody woman.* He ordered another pint and tried to come up with a valid reason for another visit to Lanchester.

***

Late afternoon on Tuesday, Beth was relaxing in the armchair in her studio, putting the final touches to her latest creation, a replica of the little hankie that she'd had plenty of time to study while Bridget had been telling her the tale of young Bessie Ellis. Because she was working from memory, she wasn't sure she'd got it exactly right. Still, she thought, it's close enough and almost as pretty. Like the pendant, which she now wore constantly, this was a piece of work she would keep.

Chapter Fifty-Six

We didn't see him again, Tinker, did we Pickie? And I never got to see Mrs Bull either. But, you know, Pickie, in those last moments I comforted meself' knowin' that I'd done somethin' good. Made somethin' beautiful. And I wouldn't be leavin' that world havin' achieved nowt. Mebbe there'd be somethin' for somebody to remember me by one day. It was a strange thought to have Pickie, when we were both bein' battered and kicked.

Chapter Fifty-Seven

Harold had come up with what he considered a valid reason to visit Beth so he left the office early on the pretext of having a new property to look over. He stopped off at a wine merchant's, and splashed out on a more expensive bottle of red wine on the recommendation of the shop owner. It was a bit more than he'd intended to pay but, what the hell, hopefully she'd be impressed. Passing Hotel Chocolat, he considered adding some special chocolates to accompany the wine but decided he'd leave that for another day. He'd spent enough on the bloody bottle. As he had last time, Harold stopped off on the way to top himself up with some Dutch courage. And, as he had that first time, he downed a couple of pints and a double whisky chaser, followed by a squirt of breath freshener before getting back on the road.

**

Beth laid the hankie aside and moved across to the garage, sighing at the sight of the remainder of the unopened boxes. She hadn't realised there were so many but if she was to get them upstairs and onto the waiting shelves she'd better get started. Bridget and Malcolm would arrive before six and the least she could do would be to half-empty each box in order to make them light enough to carry. Pickie had remained on his bed in the studio but she still heard the low growl before the sound of the car coming up the drive. 'Quiet, Pickie,' she ordered as she went to the door just in time to see Harold getting out of the car clutching a wrapped bottle of something or other. It seemed the unpacking was going to have to wait.

'Hello, Harold,' she said as he approached, then 'What can I do for you?' She hoped the formality in the question would indicate, in a not too unfriendly way, that unexpected visits weren't to be encouraged. 'I'm rather busy,' she added.

'I hope you don't mind, Beth, but I'm after a bit of advice and you're the only person who might have the lowdown. Do you think you can spare me a few minutes while I pick your brains?'

Only slightly intrigued, Beth moved aside, and said, 'I'm not sure what possible advice I could give you, but come on up and let me know what the problem is.' She moved aside and Harold walked upstairs ahead of her. Pickie remained closely at her heels as she followed him up.

Once in the lounge, Harold handed over the bottle saying, 'Thought we could share a glass or two of this. I went into that place near the cathedral and bought it on the manager's recommendation.'

'It's a bit early for me, Harold, and I do have a lot to do, but I suppose one glass won't hurt, as you've made such an effort.' She went into the kitchen to bring a couple of glasses and a corkscrew, having noted that the wine didn't have the usual screw top. She returned to see Harold settled on the sofa, eyeing Pickie who was a few feet away, half-sitting and half-crouching, looking ready to pounce. Beth opened and poured the glasses of wine before sitting herself in the armchair opposite. She called Pickie to her side. 'Now, what was it you wanted to ask me, Harold?'

Chapter Fifty-Eight

Not yet, Pickie. Let him get settled. Remember he let me get settled before he turned. Led me to believe I was just there to do the cleanin' and cookin'. And nowt else. Bert Sadler was wily. Lulled me into a false sense of security. Are you watchin', Bert? Can you see that he's got your vices? Lust and drink. Just the same. He even looks like you. That'll make it easier for us. You saw the meekness in me, didn't you. When you came to collect the rent from me da, you knew just by lookin' at me that I wasn't one for complainin'. You pretended to be kind. But you weren't. Tinker was kind and you put the fear of God into him. But you were scared, weren't you? Scared he'd run off with me. Couldn't believe that a boy could be kind to a girl without wantin' to do the fiddlin' with her. Tinker's young'un's kind. He cares for me bonnie the way Tinker cared about me. He saw how you treated me. Bossin' and orderin' me around like you owned me. That wasn't right. People shouldn't be owned. And then takin' what you really wanted from the start. Well, he'll not get his filthy hands on me bonnie. His big, cruel, graspin' hands, the same as yours which you used on me.

Chapter Fifty-Nine

'I wanted to pick your brains about Brian Jessop and anything else you can tell me about the management and staff in the London office. You see, Beth, I know Martin was an exceptional manager and I doubt I can fully live up to his legacy, but I think with a bit of hard work I can become his successor. I also know this must be a sensitive subject for you but the more I know the better the chance I have. I couldn't think of anybody else who might have inside knowledge of the people I need to try to persuade. I hope you don't mind.'

Beth did mind. The pain of losing Martin was still raw, but at least, she supposed, Harold had a genuine reason for turning up out of the blue. 'Well, I'll tell you what I can, Harold, but I'm afraid you'll find my knowledge very limited. I didn't have much to do with Martin's work other than attending the odd get-together for one reason or another. What are you hoping to find out?'

'Anything you can tell me, but mainly, who do you think is the main decision-maker? What sort of person they might be looking for. What can I do to make the right impression? And do you think there's a danger of Jessop taking over, or do you think he'd be reluctant to come north? General advice, I suppose. Anything at all, really.'

Beth wondered what she could possibly say. She really had nothing to give him and, even if she did, would she want to help him knowing how important the branch was to the futures of Bridget and Malcolm. And besides, she didn't welcome the attention Harold was giving to her legs, and other parts of her for that matter. She said the only thing that came into her mind, having noticed his somewhat crumpled and cheap-looking suit.

'Don't think me rude, Harold, but the first thing I'd recommend is a new suit. What they'll be keen to see is a particular level of professionalism in the way you dress. First impressions count from my experience.' She smiled, hoping it would take the edge of what might have come across as unwelcome criticism. 'I hope you're not offended, Harold. It's just an observation.'

'Not at all,' he answered, but aware that he did feel a twinge of resentment at what she'd said. She knew bugger all about his current situation and lack of funds. He reached across, picked up the bottle of wine and topped up his glass. Beth had only taken a couple of sips and declined his offer to top her up as well.

'Good advice,' Harold said after a large swig. 'What can you tell me about the likelihood of Brian Jessop being put in charge?'

It hadn't escaped Beth's notice, due to the slightly hardened look thrown in her direction, that he'd taken exception to her comment about his suit. 'I'm afraid I only met Jessop a few times and don't really know him, so it's really impossible for me to comment. All I can tell you is that before Martin left to come here, he thought that if he declined the position, the next person it would be offered to would be Brian. Whether he'd have accepted or not I really can't say.'

Harold had downed his second glass of wine and leant forward to once again refill his glass. Having taken a slurp, he looked directly into Beth's eyes, unsmiling, and said, 'Can't tell me much, can you! Ah well, it was worth a try and it's always good to see you, Beth. In fact, I think about you a lot, you know. Too bloody much if I'm truthful. I was hoping to persuade you to let me take you out to dinner sometime. Get to know each other better. And I'm sure you could do with a good night out after all that's happened.' He shuffled along the sofa to be nearer to Beth. She felt herself going into a panic. Pickie had risen from lying at her side to sitting watching Harold.

'Don't suppose you've got another bottle somewhere, have you?' Harold said, pouring the last of the wine. 'I'm sure you must keep a supply for that sister of yours. She seems to be partial to glass or two.'

Beth was getting seriously worried. Harold had started slurring his words, an indication that the wine he'd drunk wasn't the first of the day. The last thing she wanted was to have to cope with a lecherous drunk. She stood up and said, 'I'm sorry, Harold, but I'd like you to leave now if you don't mind. As I told you when you arrived, I'm in the middle of something I need to get on with.' She walked down the stairs and opened the front door, hoping he would follow. She noticed that Pickie hadn't followed her down as he usually did. Harold came down the stairs, stumbling slightly, with Pickie following, as though ushering him out. Reaching the bottom, where Beth was holding open the door, Harold made a sudden lunge, grabbed Beth's arm and pulled her into the studio where he thrust her against the workbench.

'Think you're too high and mighty for the likes of me, don't you,' he snarled. 'Fucking cock-teaser, that's all you are. And to think I had you down as something special.'

Beth was petrified as he pinned her arms to her sides and pushed himself against her. She was aware of the table pressing into her lower back. As she tried to scream, a look of absolute horror transformed Harold's face. He was no longer seeing Beth. He was seeing a parody of the gentle, soft Beth he'd lusted after. He wanted to back away but found it impossible. He began lashing out, punching and kicking in the effort to rid himself of the nightmarish vision before him, the wild hair, the gaping jaw, and the empty eye sockets. At the same time, a fiendish, vindictive cackle rang in his ears. His fists weren't meeting flesh. They were meeting bone. He wanted to run. The fear he felt was all-consuming but, try as he might, he couldn't take a step back. What the fuck was happening?

Beth could barely feel the punches. She was too focused on the absolute terror on Harold's face. What could he be seeing to cause such abject fear? He was looking at her as though she was the most terrifying thing he'd ever seen. He'd stopped hitting her and she tried to push him away. But he continued leaning in, pressing her painfully against the bench, still pinning her by her arms.

Chapter Sixty

You can do it now, Pickie! Sadler's for you. Didn't I tell you I'd let you have him. Let you finally have your revenge on him what saw us done for. Him what kicked you to death when you tried to save me. Left off his batterin' of me to lay into you with his boots. I tried to pull him off you, Pickie. He just shoved me aside and carried on kickin' you until you stopped movin'. Seein' you lyin' there, bleedin' and barely breathin', broke my heart so much that I wanted to die along with you. I didn't care any more. Me life was no longer worth livin'. At that moment, I hated Bert Sadler with a hate that I never thought anybody could feel. I goaded him. For the first time in my life I fought back, cursin' him and all his kin. Swearin' that even death wouldn't quell me hatred. And it hasn't.

Chapter Sixty-One

No matter how hard he tried, Harold couldn't let go of the aberration in front of him. The festering mass of disintegrating flesh and bone was repulsive beyond his wildest imagination but he couldn't unclench his hands. The hands that had turned into claws and were gripping the skeletal remains of what should have been Beth's upper arms. He closed his eyes against the monstrosity, flinching and gagging from the vile stench that was permeating his nostrils.

Beth was using all her strength but couldn't push Harold away, and the look of absolute horror on Harold's face was the most frightening thing she'd ever witnessed. She thought she heard a car pull into the drive and just managed to utter an almost inaudible, 'Help' as she felt her knees weaken and her body begin to slump towards the floor. She was only held upright by Harold's grip.

A savage snarl emanated from Pickie. His drooling jaws gaped as he leapt at Harold, whose grip was finally broken, causing him to fall backwards, eyes closed and arms flailing in an attempt to ward off the savage attack. He tried to curl into a ball as the mad animal first tore at his legs and arms before going for his throat. As he lay breathing his last, feeling the warmth of his blood seeping through his shirt as it ran freely from his jugular, he thought he heard Beth saying, with a viciousness he would never have thought possible, *For you, Bert Sadler.*

Chapter Sixty-Two

See, Sadler. See what your evil doin's brought upon your kin. You were an infection that travelled down through the generations. It's done now. Unless there are more of you. If there are, our yew tree will bring them to us eventually and the same will be done to them. His death was grisly, as we wanted it to be. Me and Pickie. His poisonous blood's stopped flowin' now. There's nowt can be done for him. Is he with you in hell yet? If not, he's on his way and he'll be with you soon. This world is rid of you. You're the cause of this festerin' hatred I have inside me. You buried me within the arms of the death tree. You didn't know you were givin' her a gift. She was grateful for the gift of us and gave us a gift in return. The gift of vengeance. I didn't have this hunger in me. Not then. Not until I was held by the yew. The yew has no forgiveness in her. She witnessed what was done to us and she embraced us. I was never embraced before. Not with love. I was clasped. But clasped for selfish purposes. Not through affection. The festerin' grew and grew within me like a sizzlin' red hot boil that wouldn't heal until lanced. It got bigger and bigger as my flesh and bones rotted and became one with the yew. The day that saw the both of us done by your great thumpin' fist and clod-hoppin' boots, I was accepting of the end of us. I thought there was nowt to be done. But she knew better. Our yew has the wisdom of her years. She used her ancient knowledge. She found a purpose in us, and her nurturing learnt us that hate and vengeance was the way to ensure renewal. She's endowed us with a second chance in return for doin' her biddin'. Well, it's done. We're back here now. Here to enjoy what was denied us by you and the others. She's promised us many years before she'll draw us back. Are you jealous? Sufferin' down there in the inferno bein' poked by devils as you burn? I'm goin' now. The hatin's leavin' me. I'm Bessie Ellis again. Gentle,

Chapter Sixty-Three

Without a collar to grab, Malcolm knew he risked Pickie turning on him, but he had to do something. He grabbed Pickie by the scruff of the neck and pulled him off Harold, Pickie instantly becoming docile once more. Kneeling down and seeing the amount of blood that was even now beginning to pool and coagulate on the tiles, Malcolm knew there was little he could do. But he had to try. He quickly pulled off his jacket and pushed it firmly against the wound in Harold's neck in an attempt to stem any more blood from pouring from Harold's neck, at the same time listening to Bridget's phone call to the emergency services. Beth was slumped on the floor, the bruises on her arms and face evident.

Epilogue

It's been more than eighteen months now since the last of them. Can I say the last? I don't think there'll be any more. At least I hope not. Three unfortunate incidents are surely enough. I'm sitting here in my studio watching the lengthening shadow of the solitary yew cast by the sun as it sinks over the moors. Those few short months took their toll on my health for a while, especially with Chris and James trying to insist that the house is cursed. I never believed that. I think it's blessed. I think what's happened has strengthened me. Pickie couldn't be found after that day, which is just as well because I think he'd have had to be put down. But he's always by my side when I'm alone. I don't know how he does it, but he disappears if anyone else is around. Anyone but Malcolm, that is. Malcolm visits often. He's always willing to lend a hand with the sort of problem that sometimes arises in a house this size. In exchange he uses my garage to work on his projects. He's taking a course in metalwork and always has something on the go. Always tinkering. I tease him sometimes by calling him Tinker. He doesn't seem to mind. Always smiling, that's Malcolm. He decided he didn't want to be an estate agent once Brian Jessop took over. Apart from Bridget, none of the original team are there now.

Chris and James are getting married next month and we're going to be neighbours. I think she wants to keep an eye on me. Make sure I'm all right. I keep trying to convince her that I'm fine. In fact, I can't remember ever being so content. There's a voice in my head that tells me what's past is past. Done with. Chris finds it difficult to believe that I'm happy sitting here in this house which has seen so much tragedy. I find it easy to lose myself in my needlework. She tries to get me to go out more. But I've improved a lot. I suppose my health suffered a bit for a while but I'm fully recovered now apart from the pain in my left foot which sometimes makes me limp. The doctors can't find the cause, believing it to be psychosomatic. A side-effect of the trauma. So I'm just going to have to live with it. Anyway, it doesn't bother me too much. Another side-effect is that I have what I can only describe as memories of another time. False, I know, but persistent nevertheless. The nicest one finds me sitting sewing in the corner of a laundry chatting to Bridget. I think the tale of Bessie embedded itself in my head. But it's not unpleasant. More like a daydream, really. Recently I find myself smiling more. Singing, even. I feel a sort of freedom. I feel reborn.

THE END